FOREVER - PART 2

THE STORY OF LIAM AND ROXIE

LISA PHILLIPS

eBook ISBN: 979-8-88552-181-9

Paperback ISBN: 979-8-88552-182-6

Published by Two Dogs Publishing, LLC. Idaho, USA

Cover Design by Sasha Almazan and Gene Mollica, GS Cover Design Studio, LLC

Edited by Meghan Kleinschmidt of Literary Pearl Editing

ONE

"You need to eat something." His voice sounded like gravel shifting underfoot. The kind of vocal damage that came from an extended period of screaming.

Still, underneath it, Roxie could faintly hear her brother.

The boy he'd been—Adam Helton.

Beside her now was Angus Dubkowsky, per his driver's license. The man who had picked her up from outside the hospital after she found out Liam had been killed in that compound explosion.

Dead.

Roxie stared at the ocean. The boat rocked back and forth, back and forth. But the lullaby of the still water, the sky that stretched overhead, and the gradual bleed of one day into the next did nothing to soothe her. "I want my dog."

"There's work to do. Millions of lives are at stake, and you're worried about your dog?"

"She's all the family I have left." Roxie turned to him.

The expression on his face didn't shift. His beard

growth covered what she knew was a thick scar on the left side of his face. His right forearm had some knotted scars on the top and the underside, the same spot protection dogs were taught to grasp the assailant and hang on.

Despite her jab about their family status, he remained completely impassive. He might as well have been made of stone. Maybe he was.

"What do you think a dog is gonna do on a boat?" He folded his arms. "They need grass. They need to run."

"Have you even had a dog since you left?"

His jaw flexed. "My life isn't conducive to having a dog underfoot."

Roxie unfolded her legs from the chair and stood. "Then you need to change your life because there's something wrong with it."

"We have a lead."

She flinched. That seemed to happen a lot, lately. But then, she'd had everything she'd ever wanted. And in a matter of days, it was gone. When her brother picked her up, along with several of his men, they'd cleaned out the hotel room she'd shared with Liam nearby but only brought her things—and no electronics.

The boat was a safehouse for them. Just not one that was big enough she could get privacy except when they left her alone on the deck.

Someone had offered her a *drink*, but alcohol wasn't going to numb the pain, and she would end up feeling worse than she already did.

They had Carim below deck. She pretended she couldn't hear the sound of them...extracting...information from him.

Adam said, "He asked again to talk to you."

Roxie looked at the water. It wasn't like anyone had given her a phone so she could call the Northwest Counter Terrorism Taskforce office number. Make sure she still had a job with them. Get her dog back. She hadn't been able to connect to the camera that showed her if Pronto was recovering from getting kicked. It felt like more than just a couple of weeks ago now.

More like another lifetime.

Thinking about it just made her think of Liam, and that hurt too much to do. She would rather be numb, but that wasn't working either. Instead, it felt like a void. Or a rubber band pulled so tight she didn't want to do anything to snap it.

"Simon cares about you."

Roxie said, "So we're just going to continue glossing over the fact you guys are some super-secret black ops Vanguard team that no one knows about. And I worked there for months. I've never even heard more than a whisper of you."

"That's the way it has to be."

"So you would've let me live my entire life believing you were dead. Letting me think I had no family. Completely alone. No one to walk me down the aisle."

"Simon told me you went to the courthouse. I wouldn't have been able to get back in time." He lifted his head. "He sent me a photo. I thought you looked happy, and I was happy for you. Until I saw you guys for myself, and I realized he was no different than that other guy."

Roxie slapped her open palm across his face.

Her brother just stood there. He did nothing to stop her when they both know he could have.

"He was nothing like Mark."

"So you say." He lifted his chin slightly.

"I'm not having this conversation with you. You know nothing about me and Liam." The night breeze blew hair across her face, and she closed her eyes for a second. Every part of her wanted to remember her husband, to call forth all the good that had been between them. But using it just to prove a point with her brother wasn't what those memories were for.

The rest of her life, they were all Roxie had.

"I'll add that to the list of things not to bring up." Adam shifted his stance, little more than a shrug though he didn't move his shoulders. "Right under Simon. Vanguard. Your old life. Your job. All you wanna talk about is your dog. Well, there's a case to work. So why don't we focus up, get this done. When the threat is over, you can go find your pet."

She could've slapped him again, but Roxie's hand still hurt from the last time. What had started out as a grief reaction had turned into a reprieve from her life and the things she didn't want to face but would have to eventually. If she wasn't careful, it would turn into inertia. Like her seeming inability to open the worn Bible one of the guys had given her.

Years would go by.

Hiding might be easier, and often necessary, but she had a job. A life. Decisions. Responsibilities. She couldn't sit on the deck of this boat forever.

"What solid lead did you torture out of Carim?"

Adam shook his head. "He and I came to an agreement."

"That's what you're going to call it?"

"I'm giving you a lot of room here, but you should know more than one of my men has threatened to throw you overboard to let the water knock some sense into you. Or a shark."

"That isn't funny." Roxie folded her arms across her chest but realized that made her mannerism match his. She let her hands fall to her sides. "If I'm such an inconvenience, drop me off on shore somewhere. I'll figure it out."

Adam just stared at her.

"What?"

He let out a sigh.

There was definitely something. "Tell me."

Adam scratched at his jaw, his fingertips disappearing into the thick, dark blonde hair that now curled on his head. "Darwish put out a hit on you and Liam."

Roxie swallowed against the lump in her throat, but it didn't move. She inhaled sea air through her nostrils, not even able to appreciate what was an admittedly gorgeous night. She would have to admit that, if pressed, it was beautiful out here. The problem was that she didn't feel anything. Just...cold.

Her husband was dead, so Darwish had what he wanted. Liam had been caught in the explosion at a black site. Darwish had intended to free his brother from government confinement, but Adam and his team had intercepted, rescued her, and taken Carim for their own ends.

"Fine. I'm not safe." She didn't like the idea of being captive any more than anyone else. "I can protect myself. Darwish has a whole plan. It's not like he's going to waste much time worrying about taking me out."

"So you'd rather disappear?"

"Whatever I do, it'll be my choice."

Adam said, "How about being a pain, stopping him before he completes his plans, and proving to everyone that you can do this on your own?"

"You were doing so well. Then you ruined it." Roxie turned away and walked to the edge, grasping the railing to anchor herself in the moment. Motion. Feeling. Anything to fight the numbness and the slow creep of inertia.

"I just want you to know you're strong on your own. That you can do this, and you didn't need him."

Roxie looked at her brother, who almost looked sorry. She wasn't convinced he was capable of feeling remorse. "Except I'll be doing it with you and your team there to back me up and protect me."

At least with Liam, she'd been with the man she loved.

Roxie didn't want to regret spending all those weeks in Georgia at Marshals training. Would she even get to go and do the job? Maybe they'd assign her to some random field office. The taskforce probably wouldn't want her to work with them when they didn't get Liam anymore. He'd been the one they wanted, and she just happened to come along as well. A package deal.

"We aren't gonna crowd you."

The implication being that they—and he—weren't like "them." Which was how they described her husband, the ex who had abused her, and his brother who'd come after her. As if there was any correlation *on earth* between Liam and those guys. It was insane. They were night and day. Liam had been everything a good man was supposed to be.

But did he get a shot at a long life? Or happiness?

No.

A heavy hand landed on her shoulder, and she flinched. "Sorry." He practically grunted the word. "Help us finish this."

Roxie turned slowly, lifting her gaze to meet her brother's. "Why do you need me?"

It was the way he'd said it. Encouraging her to help them out, like she was one of the team when they had no intention of extending that invitation. Obviously, Vanguard knew where she was, but no one had spoken to her about her future.

Her friend Destiny from Benson had worked there since she was rescued from kidnapping in Africa. Her fiancé, Jasper Hollingsworth, now ran the company since Clare had decided to stay home with her new baby more. They were in transition.

Except for Simon, no one had reached out.

"Fine. We're going to draw him out, and we need someone to stand with Carim in public."

There it was. "And you can't show your faces."

"It is what it is. This is the life we've chosen."

Roxie wanted to get into that, but she was already exhausted from talking to him for this long. She needed sleep. Except even that oblivion didn't seem to help her recharge right now. "Sounds like something you tell yourself to make you feel better."

She knew something about that. Maybe it was a family trait.

Adam turned to look out over the water. "The focus is this mission. We need to stop Darwish, and that means taking Carim out with someone to watch him while we provide overwatch."

"So I'm in the line of fire while you guys are all tucked away and safe?" Roxie didn't like that idea.

"It's not like we can fake Carim's face. We don't have that tech on the boat, and it isn't a sure thing anyway. Darwish will know it's not him."

"So you parade me out there with a terrorist when you know for a fact his brother put out a hit on me?"

"Two birds and all that."

Roxie shook her head. "What?"

"We keep Carim secure. We catch Darwish when he shows up, and we eliminate the threat against you. Maybe that's three birds and one stone."

"You're pretty convinced you guys can pull this off." He didn't appear the least bit nervous. "Confident much?"

"We aren't going to let anything happen to you."

"You think I care about that?" She just wanted her dog back. Maybe when the mission was done, she could sneak off and make her way to Dakota's house. Her boss probably wanted to talk to her anyway. If there was no reason for Roxie to be protected, then she could get back to her life.

Without Liam.

The whole idea made her sick, but she also knew it was something she had to do.

No more hiding.

"Fine," Roxie said. "Let's get this done."

TWO

It had taken him an entire day to recall his name.

Things had come in pieces since then. Fragments he'd had to assemble in his mind, until something like a personality, or a history, came together.

Then she showed up.

An older woman, beautiful and serene. She'd laughed when he told her that. She'd laid her hand on his, and a tear had rolled down his cheek. Mom hadn't left his side in the three days since she'd found him.

Someone shook his shoulder gently, an intrusion into his thoughts. "Time to wake up."

Liam O'Connell blinked, and the room came slowly into focus. He sucked in a breath and looked at her, standing over his bedside. "I was just resting my eyes."

She gave him the same look she did every time he lied to her. As if he were still a little kid who exasperated her and not a grown man. "I know, Lee. But the doctor wants to look at you."

"Good." He reached over and hit the button to raise the head of the bed. "Time to get out of here."

His mom reached for his phone, but Liam grabbed it first. Which should tell her all she needed to know about his condition and the fact he would be fine.

It was time to get out of this bed and look for Roxie.

"Hey, there." The doctor smiled as she came over, probably in her forties. He'd guess she had Indian heritage, and her brown eyes were warm. Some doctors seemed jaded and insisted on treating symptoms rather than seeing them as a person. This doctor held out her hand, and Liam set his in it.

She hung on, looking at the face of her analogue watch.

He realized she was checking his pulse. And at the same time, connecting with him person-to-person in that small way. The entire staff knew his wife had been there. That he'd been caught in a catastrophic explosion, and nearly lost his life. His head still thrummed with pain even though they'd been pumping him with all kinds of meds since he landed in this place.

"I hear you're ready to get out of here."

Liam flipped his phone over and saw the notification. "I hear you're the one that has to sign off on it."

"Ah, someone willing to follow the rules."

He wasn't sure that was true, but things had been coming back slowly in the four days since he woke up. Far too long to be out of it. Especially when he remembered the last time he'd seen Roxie.

And then that empty hallway.

A dead Marine.

SUVs.

Ka-boom. His world had flipped upside down and inverted. Now he had four stitches on the left side of his head, just back from his temple, and a broken wrist they'd put a cast on. One of his toes was broken, and his hip had been bruised badly, but nothing had broken there.

"At least to a point, right?" She flashed a smile at him.

Liam pressed his lips together and smiled.

The doctor chuckled through her assessment of him, while he grunted and tried to pretend her prodding didn't make him want to hurl. His mom had brought him a smoothie hours ago. He needed a cheeseburger and the chance to get out there and look for Roxie.

His phone buzzed against his stomach.

The doctor set her stethoscope back around her shoulders. "If you insist on being upright, I'll accept you leaving, but only on the understanding you spend at least nineteen hours of every day horizontal. No exceptions. And those five hours upright are broken up through the day. I don't want you alone, just in case you run into any problems, and the moment you do, I want you on the way to the closest emergency department."

His mom nodded, standing on the other side of the bed from the doctor. "I'll look after him."

The doc gave him some more instructions and a prescription for meds, arranging for a wheelchair to get him down to the exit where his pickup would be right around the time Liam told them he was heading out.

Soon as the doctor left, he pushed the covers back and eased up to sitting. Feet over the edge. His mom just stood there. Liam sighed and glanced at her. "Fine, you're gonna have to help me."

She chuckled and crouched, tugging socks on his feet. "Some of it you can handle yourself. I'm your mama, but you're a grown man."

She set a pair of already laced sneakers on the ground. Liam stuck his feet into the shoes, ignoring the tug of pressure in his broken toe, and hiked up the sweats over his underwear. His mom turned from the bag and held out a T-shirt. Getting it over his head took some doing, and by the time they were done, he was sweating.

"Did you bring me a gun?"

His mom grinned. "Boy, who do you think I am? It's your father's pistol and his old shoulder holster." She set a hand on his shoulder. "You're about the same size."

Grief welled up like a clogged drain, rising until he had to do something or it would overflow. "Thanks, Mom."

"When I ask for your blessing, don't argue."

Liam took the holster from her and nearly dropped it and the pistol on the floor. "What?"

"Bob Davis." She straightened her shoulders. "You didn't think it was *casual*, did you?"

"I was trying not to think about it at all."

"I might be your mother, but I'm also a woman."

"Same answer." He shuddered.

His mom started to chuckle. "Conrad said the same when I told him. Rory hasn't called me back yet, but I heard he's starting *another* restaurant up in Alaska."

"Big place. Maybe they need more than one Backdraft." Changing the subject to his brothers was much better than talking about his mother's love life. "If he doesn't call you back, tell me. I'll go up there and roust him out."

"Don't wait until fire season starts. Soon as summer hits, things will heat up all over the northwest. Rory won't be reachable until every one of those fires is put out."

"I'll track him down." Because that meant he would be free too. It meant Roxie was found, too, and this whole mess had been taken care of. It meant work had calmed down so there was time to find his brother and tell him to call Mom.

Liam opened his texts and sent one to Rory right then.

Call Mom.

She patted his shoulder, and Liam got himself wheeled downstairs. Out of the elevator onto the lobby floor, Liam tried to figure out how to explain that he wasn't going with her.

She walked alongside him and didn't tell him to stay put while she went and got the car.

The exterior doors slid open, and the wheelchair bumped outside. The orderly toed down the brakes. Liam said, "Thanks."

"No problem." He took a step back.

A black SUV headed up the incline and pulled to a stop in front of him. The back door opened, and a slender Belgian Malinois hopped out, bounded over, and jumped into Liam's lap. He grunted. "Pronto."

The dog licked his face on one side, shifted and

started on the other side, including his neck all the way up to his eye. "All right." He rubbed her sides. "All right. That's gross. I already need a shower." He put his hand on the fur above her nose and eased her away from his bandage. "Thanks, Pronto."

Liam had to fight back the emotion that surprised him. He sniffed and smiled at the woman who climbed out of the SUV. Striking Native American features and a wide smile. She could be extremely threatening, but the woman Liam knew now was markedly different than the stories the others told about her.

"Dakota."

A round African American woman eased out of the front passenger seat. Gold sandals and a professional black dress.

"Talia."

Dakota lifted her chin, eying the dog. Probably ready to call Pronto off if it looked like Liam was suffering by having a dog on his lap.

Talia touched his face. "Babycakes. You're lookin' good." She kissed his cheek.

A tall African American man, bigger than Liam's wide shoulders, got out of the back. "Woman, he's injured. Dial it back."

She winked at Liam.

Liam's mom chuckled.

The two men who rounded the SUV were Niall and Josh. NCIS and DEA respectively. The taskforce packed a punch in command presence, the force of all of them in front of him a little overwhelming. A German Shepherd hopped into the front seat and put her nose to the window. Josh gave a hand signal, and the dog jumped into the rear again.

Liam blinked back sweat in his eyes.

His mom said, "Well, seems you will be in capable hands."

He frowned. He should introduce the team—

Dakota came over and gave his mom a *hug*. "We'll take very good care of him."

"And bring me back my daughter-in-law." His mom cleared her throat.

"Yes, ma'am." Dakota nodded, turning back to the assembled group.

Liam's mom crouched beside his wheelchair, her eyes sad and angry at the same time. "Find her."

He nodded. "Love you."

"I know." She touched his cheek. "Love you, too, honey. See you soon."

Liam had a hand navigating from the chair to the SUV. They let him take one of the captain's chairs in the middle row. One of those tiny water bottles, barely bigger than his palm, appeared in his hand. Then was removed. Then appeared again, the cap unsealed.

"Thanks." He cleared his throat.

Someone squeezed his shoulder. Niall spoke softly in the backseat. "Yeah, babe. We got him." He paused. "We will. Love you."

Talia's husband Mason, not part of the team but here nonetheless, sat beside Liam. Talia had the front seat, where Josh drove, which put Dakota behind him. The DEA K-9 in the back, likely tucked in her crate.

Josh turned from the parking lot onto the street, rocking the vehicle enough that Pronto turned in a circle between the middle row chairs and laid down with her muzzle on his shoe. Liam managed to reach far enough to pet her side for a second. "Someone start talking. I want to know where Roxie is."

In the front seat, Talia let out a sigh. The others exchanged glances.

Liam wasn't going to ask again, and not just because he was the newest hire. Lowest on the ladder.

Dakota reached forward and squeezed his shoulder. "You know she was taken by Carim. We have some intel that indicates the SUVs met a helicopter two miles from the compound, where there was a shootout, and the men who took Carim were killed. The occupants of the helicopter took both Carim and Roxie."

Talia said, "Any footage or evidence from the compound was all destroyed in the explosion. We have no idea where she went, or what happened to her. The government agents that arrived acting as 'police' and local law enforcement didn't come up as any agency or department even we've heard of."

"So anyone who responded to the explosion was a spy or some other kind of covert agent."

"Or black ops," Niall said.

Mason glanced at him, then told Liam, "I pressed some of my contacts, but no one will tell me who they are. No one even knew about the explosion. It hasn't been on the news. It's no surprise you showed up at the hospital as one of a handful of John Does."

Liam rubbed his cast along his breastbone, trying to relieve the ache. "So she's been who-knows-where for more than a week, and Darwish probably has his brother back. The plan is still on."

Dakota cleared her throat. "There's more."

THREE

Roxie got out of the van, holding the door for Carim. He seemed able bodied enough. "Come on. Let's get this over with."

He looked through her to their surroundings. The city park in the middle of downtown that Adam, or Darwish, or both, had chosen for their meeting seemed like an oasis of green in the middle of bustling humanity. The perfect place to set off an explosive device that would cripple the city and terrorize the people who lived here.

"This way." Roxie ran her arm along her right hip, comforted by the feel of the gun under her jacket. Thankfully, it was cool enough she didn't look odd wearing layers. The rest of her was haggard. She knew that.

She'd tied the top half of her hair back off her face. No makeup. What was the point? This was an operation. It wasn't about what she looked like, even though the note of disappointment in herself was there. She was still a *girl*. Even if she was also a Marine, a US Marshal, an operator, an investigator, and a widow.

The thoughts were only distractions, though. She needed to focus up.

Carim walked alongside her.

"I'm surprised you haven't tried to run off already."

His arms hung by his sides. Maybe his steps were a function of how long it had been since he felt free. Kept for years by the government in a black site. Held on a boat for days below decks. Until he'd come to some sort of compromise—or so Adam claimed.

Her brother hadn't fully explained this to her, but she could guess. *We wait for Darwish to show up and try to rescue his brother. We take him down.* As if that was all of it. She knew what it looked like when he lied, at least back when he'd been in high school.

Sneaking out and then lying to their dad when he got caught.

It looked a lot different now. His life the last ten-plus years hadn't been peaceful. Adam was barely the boy she'd known. But he still thought she couldn't tell when he wasn't speaking the whole truth?

"I understand my role here," Carim said.

He'd been almost cocky when those men had extracted him from the black site. He had planned to give her over to his rescuers as a reward. Instead, Adam and his men had killed them and taken Carim.

"And what is that?"

"The same as yours." He glanced at her, turning and stopping in the center of the park beside a fountain. "Bait."

Roxie stuck her thumbs in her jeans pockets. It was part of her job that her life might be on the line on occasion, even every day sometimes. What else was new? Except for the fact that right now, she had a whole lot less to lose than she used to.

A woman jogged past them, earbuds in. She didn't even glance their way.

Two dogs wrestled each other on the grass. A young man, probably late teens, tossed a ball, and they abandoned the battle with each other to chase after it.

Above the low buzz of traffic, she could hear birds, and kids laughing. Things she hadn't heard on the boat. Signs of life she'd missed.

The numbness that had been creeping didn't seem so cold in the light of day, surrounded by people. Just the fact of their being nearby was enough to move her heart to beat just a little. Roxie wasn't ready to connect. Standing here was enough.

"Heads up." The voice came through her earpiece. "Possible shooter, northwest corner on the roof of the bank building."

Roxie kept watching at ground level, not drawing anyone's attention to the place one of Adam's men pointed out.

Someone replied, "Copy that. Checking it out now."

Beside her, Carim shifted. "Is something happening I should be aware of?"

She eyed him, not all the way convinced by his demeanor. "I was just wondering why you're going along with this."

"I needed to stretch my legs. Of course."

Yeah, that wasn't it. "And your brother?"

"We have not seen each other in many years. I have no idea where he is or what he's doing."

"But you weren't surprised that he was going to

rescue you from that black site." She crossed her arms. "Were you?"

"Call it...wishful thinking." He scanned their surroundings as much as she did. Placid and calm, as if she was supposed to believe this wasn't his shot at leaving.

"And now?" She shrugged. "Why not just run?"

"Your brother has ensured I will not."

Roxie frowned. "What does that mean?" Did her brother have a shooter trained on Carim in case he ran for it? They could hit her, whoever they were. His men had tier one training, but that didn't mean they would never make a mistake.

Carim unzipped his jacket, sliding the zipper down just a couple of inches. Enough for her to see the wire.

Roxie took a step back.

Carim's teeth flashed in a kind of smile. "Indeed." The zipper went back up.

"He's going to blow up you...and Darwish?" Roxie's hands curled into fists, tucked under her elbows. The muscles in her shoulders became as flexible as concrete.

In her earpiece, she heard someone say, "When she puts it like *that*, it doesn't sound good."

Adam replied, "All I heard is that there will be two less terrorists in the world. I'm not sure what the problem is."

So her brother had declared himself to be judge, jury, and executioner? "Is that what you do?" She glanced aside, so Carim wouldn't mistake her words as being directed at him. "Take lives, risk others, and make the choice whether someone lives or dies?"

She wouldn't have thought Vanguard was the

kind of company that would allow it. Then again, these guys were rogue at best. Renegades, they'd called themselves. She didn't know whether to shake their hands or call the police. But contacting Vanguard meant reconnecting with her life. Facing her loss and the pain of it, coming face to face with sympathy and grief.

Not ready.

They needed to just finish this so she could leave Adam and his friends to do whatever they wanted. She would be able to get Pronto and figure out what to do next, and he could carry on. Assuming she wasn't somehow supposed to be a note of conscience for a group of men who could push boundaries too far. Until there were no boundaries at all.

She didn't want the role of overseer, but God might just have led her into the position He wanted her to be in before she even realized she needed it.

These men weren't her safety net.

There was nothing safe about them at all.

Across the park, a driver honked their horn at another vehicle. A van cut someone off, going fast. In her earpiece, she heard two shots. They sounded far away to her other ear but audible enough she glanced up at that rooftop.

A second later, someone said, "Threat neutralized."

"Think that's the only one, boss?"

Adam said, "Keep your eyes open. The van is circling, and I have eyes on some players. Could be who Darwish sent to get his brother."

Roxie wanted to scream at them—or tear out the earpiece and run. She stomped her boots and looked around, determined to provide at least some control over the situation. This could so easily spin out in ways she wouldn't be able to account for.

A couple walked together, about a half mile away right now. Someone else shifted, but by the time she looked, they'd gone behind a tree. Hair on the back of her neck tingled, and her stomach did that odd thing that wasn't quite nausea. An indication that things were about to kick off.

"Heads up."

Carim glanced over. Adam said, "What is it?"

Roxie couldn't quantify it as anything in particular. She kept scanning, watching for another shooter or something else. *Lord, help me see clearly.* She realized then that she'd hardly spoken to God since the compound. Since the last time she saw Liam.

She'd worked hard to cultivate a relationship with Him that was separate from her husband. The two didn't need to mix together. Liam might've been her hero, but he had never been her savior. She would need God if she was going to navigate the rest of her life.

Help me, please.

She didn't know what to pray more than that but knew it was okay.

The call came through her earpiece. "Ambush. Ambush. Ambu—"

Metal slammed into metal. The sharp deafening thud of a car hitting another car. Roxie spun to where their van was parked and saw a truck had hit the back of it. She turned back to Carim. "We need to—"

His body jerked, and he grabbed for his knee at the same time his legs gave out. The terrorist fell to the ground and hit hard.

Someone screamed. People in the park started to run.

"Get him out of there, Rox!" Adam's order was nothing short of a command, and one she was expected to follow without question.

Roxie grabbed Carim under the arms, mostly grasping his jacket, and started to drag him toward the nearest tree. Those around her not running immediately became worthy of suspicion.

Another shot rang out. Who was shooting?

A chip flung out from the fountain and hit her in the arm, nothing but a shard that had ricocheted where the round hit the concrete. It sliced across her skin. Roxie cried out but didn't stop dragging Carim to safety.

"Cover! She needs cover!"

Roxie focused on her task, rather than the thought that something had happened to whoever was supposed to have been protecting her.

She let go of Carim and he slumped by the tree. The bullet had hit his thigh, taking a chunk of his leg as it passed through. He wasn't going anywhere. She spoke into her radio. "Tell me his vest isn't going to detonate before I can get clear."

Carim grunted, both hands on his leg.

"Busy right now." Adam sounded breathless.

"Do you see Darwish?" She hadn't spotted him or an invading force like the one at the compound. They were all dead, but Darwish could've hired more people.

Roxie got the sense there was someone behind her. She turned in time to see Niall O'Caran, her taskforce teammate, behind her. He said, "Looks like you might need some help."

Behind him, she spotted movement.

Running toward her across the grass. Roxie's whole body stilled. Time seemed to stop. Pronto raced across the grass, and the fur missile slammed into Roxie. She fell backward, one leg bent under her, not realizing until she had to gasp a breath that she was sobbing. Crying.

She held onto the dog, who tried to burrow as close to her as possible. Roxie rubbed the dog's sides and then wiped her face with her jacket sleeve. "Pronto." She had to clear her throat. "I know. I know. I missed you."

The yelling in her earpiece intruded into everything, nearly overdriving the channel. She winced and pulled it out, then said to Niall. "He needs help." She didn't know what she needed.

Niall held out his hand. "Let me help *you*. That's why we're here."

She clasped his wrist, and he hauled her to her feet, steadying her with a hand on her elbow. Pronto leaned against her leg, doing circles around her. "The team is here?"

Relief washed over her.

"You're safe now." Niall turned to look over his shoulder.

Roxie didn't know what that meant. "I'm glad you guys are here, but—"

Across the grass, Adam shoved another man back. *Liam.*

FOUR

Liam nearly fell but refused to let the angry man in front of him knock him down. "Guess your luck ran out, then."

"You shouldn't have come." Adam Helton glared at him, about to come in for another strike. Which, considering the rest of Liam's team was close, would be a bad idea. Roxie's brother said, "She was better off with you dead."

Liam wanted to ask what that meant but spotted her headed for him at a flat out run. He moved to meet her, but Adam got in front of him.

"Get out of the way."

Roxie screamed, "Adam, move!"

Her brother's face hardened. Roxie shoved him out of the way and slammed into Liam, tears running down her face. He wrapped his arms around her, and she clung to him the way he'd seen her do with Pronto a second ago.

"Thank You, Jesus. Thank You, Lord." Her grasp shifted, as if she didn't know what to hang onto. "You're alive. You're alive." As if she didn't quite believe what she was saying. Or feeling.

Liam held onto her, while over her shoulder he kept watch. Protecting her. Letting her process what she was feeling.

Her brother glared at them, a rifle clipped to the front of his vest. Earpiece in. Niall crouched by the tree where Carim complained loudly about his leg.

Dakota.

Josh, who'd wrangled Pronto with his dog and had them both leashed again.

The team was back together.

He and Roxie were back together. Liam turned his head to her neck and breathed, giving himself a moment he would expand on later. When they were alone. Then he said, "Someone needs to tell me what's going on."

Roxie shifted so he could see her face but didn't let go of him.

Liam swiped her cheeks with his thumbs. The things her brother had said came back to his mind. *Better off when you were dead.* Seeing Roxie's brother here had given him the first indication this meeting wasn't going to be a routine operation.

The taskforce had uncovered an exchange going down here today between Darwish and some unknown party—a clandestine group they believed to be the ones who had taken Carim and Roxie from the compound.

Then he'd seen the two of them in the middle of the park.

All the reasonable thoughts had left his head, along with the desire to comply with Dakota's order to stay in the van. He'd spotted one of Adam's operators jump from their van and run down the sidewalk after...something...and climbed into the front seat. He'd slammed their vehicle into Adam's.

Liam absorbed the shock and grief in her expression. He held onto her, his palms on the warm skin of her neck. Either side. Feeling her pulse. Feeling her in his arms. "I'm right here."

She sobbed and leaned in. At the last second, before their lips met, she jerked her head around to her brother and pointed a finger at him. "Disarm that device!"

Liam stiffened.

"Adam!"

"Fine." Her brother whirled around on his boots and stomped toward Carim and Niall.

"A device?"

"He wired up Carim with an explosive—that's not what I want to talk to you about!"

Liam tugged her closer and held her tight. "You're safe now."

"I know." She shook her head, more tears rolling down her cheeks. "I thought you were dead."

He frowned, which made pain thrum through his skull. Liam worked his jaw in a yawn, but it didn't help much.

Roxie's gaze drifted to the bandage on the side of his head. "What happened to you? Was it the compound explosion?"

"You thought I was dead?" When she nodded, he said, "I was unidentified, but when I woke up in the hospital after a while, I remembered who I was. I called you."

"I lost my phone when the compound exploded. Carim was there, and then my brother. I went back after the explosion, and they said you were already at the hospital, but when I went there, they said you were dead." She hiccupped and sniffed. "I thought you were dead."

Liam shook his head. "There must have been a mix-up. I thought you'd been kidnapped. I came here today because we were going to rescue you."

Roxie got as close as she could. "You did." She held on tight. "You always do."

Liam squeezed his eyes shut. He'd missed hearing that. Being together was more right than being apart ever would be. "I can't believe you thought I was dead."

She shuddered in his arms.

"The team didn't hear from you."

She lifted her gaze to meet his. "I wasn't ready to call them. I wanted to get Pronto from Dakota, but Adam told me we had to do this first."

There was more to it, and they'd have to talk through all of it to get it settled. "Are you okay?"

"With you here, yes. With my brother hanging me out as bait with Carim? Not so much." She glanced around. "There was a shooter. Someone hit Carim in the leg."

Liam put his arm around her shoulders, and they walked to the rest of the team. Dakota strode over, along with Josh. All of them in their federal agent jackets, and Josh had a ball cap on. He handed the leash for Pronto to Roxie.

She said, "Thanks."

He nodded. "Good to see you. She's doing a lot better."

Roxie flushed. "I can see that."

Liam didn't let go of his wife. He probably would be able to at some point, but right now, that wasn't an option. Not after waking up and having days not knowing if she was all right. If she was alive.

What was happening to her.

She shifted the leash so her hand was through the loop and held onto his arm. He felt wetness between his fingers and looked down. "You're bleeding."

Adam straightened fast, turning away from Carim. "We need an ambulance anyway." He looked at Roxie's arm. "That's just a scratch." He dug in his thigh pocket in his cargoes and handed Liam a package. Gauze with a powder on it that would make her wound clot and stop bleeding.

Liam tore open the packet.

Roxie held her arm out. "Is the device disarmed?"

Adam said, "Would we all be standing here if it wasn't?"

"Explain to me how this situation isn't all your doing." Roxie stood her ground, even if it was in Liam's embrace.

Liam liked that a whole lot. His wife had a backbone, and she had the strength to stand for herself. But she also relied on him—needed him.

"You said Darwish would come." Roxie shrugged one shoulder. "So where is he?"

Dakota shifted her weight. "I have the same question. I don't believe we've been introduced, but I know who you are."

"Great," Adam said. His attention shifted to the side for a second. "Copy that."

Liam shifted Roxie to his other side so he was between her and Adam. "What's going on?"

Her brother knew exactly what that move meant. "There was a shooter. We took care of it. But that was before someone took a pot shot at Carim. Care to explain that one?"

Dakota shook her head. "It wasn't any of us. Maybe your men missed someone. Or there's a traitor on your team."

Adam tipped his head back and barked a rusty laugh that lasted as long as a single heartbeat. Then he said nothing.

Apparently that reaction was enough.

Dakota said, "We will be taking Carim into custody."

"Want me to laugh again?" He glared at all of them, but especially Liam.

Roxie said, "Did you know Liam was alive?"

Adam shrugged. "I didn't look into it. I don't have people behind computers checking."

"Except you do," she told him pointedly. "So, did Simon want to tell me that Liam was alive?"

"It was you who didn't want to speak to him."

Liam clenched down on his back teeth. "Are we going to go around and around about this all day, or are you going to admit you lied?" Even if it was by omission, it was still a lie.

Adam said, "None of you know me. You don't have the right to judge anything I say or do." His gaze shifted again. "I have to go. My men need backup."

He didn't wait around. He rushed off, quickly moving to a sprint.

Sirens in the distance approached the park. Probably their team had decided to split before the authorities turned up so they could continue to live in the shadows.

"Nice guy." Niall looked over his shoulder.

"Carim needs a doctor, fast. He's losing a lot of blood."

Dakota said, "Almost here."

The sirens grew louder, sounding now like police and an ambulance. Liam's team would have to coordinate with law enforcement and figure out what happened here. Whatever truth they decided on, it wouldn't match the fact that, like Liam, Roxie had a hit out on her. And her brother had put her in the line of fire to get the result he wanted.

Liam wasn't even sure what that result was.

Pronto shifted to lean against both their legs. Liam said, "Let's go find somewhere to sit." Like the van—if he hadn't wrecked it.

Josh whistled.

Liam caught the keys to the SUV that Weber tossed to him. "Thanks."

Neither he nor Roxie let go of each other, their arms around each other's waists. Her head on his shoulder all the way to the vehicle, where he held the door for her, and they climbed onto the backseat so they could sit close on the bench. Despite the stitches on the side of his head, the fact his toe hurt like crazy and the other bruises and aches, he was alive. That was what counted.

She turned to him, touching his cheeks. "I can't believe you're here."

Liam kissed her like he never had. Like it would be the last time. As if it was necessary then to pour every ounce of feeling he had into it.

Some minutes later, he didn't care how long it had been, she pulled back, breathing hard.

"I'm glad I am alive."

She smiled, and he heard her breathy exhale.

"God kept you safe while I couldn't."

She nodded. "And sane. Though, barely. I was about to lose it and turn into some kind of movie action figure bent on revenge. It was touch and go."

Liam kissed her cheek.

The ambulance had pulled in front of the SUV. He could see the open rear doors, where they loaded Carim on a stretcher into the back.

"Darwish never showed up."

Liam said, "Unless Adam's guys had him, and just didn't tell us."

"He would've blown up Carim and hopefully his brother, too, if they got away. Maybe as a last resort." She shook her head. "Is there at least a part of you that wants to quit this case, let the team take care of it, and drive off into the sunset?"

Pronto groaned and rolled onto her back between the middle row seats, her front paws in the air. Totally content. Safe. Her family back together. All was right in her world.

Liam answered honestly. "Yes."

Problem was, going away to get some time together was what had started this whole thing in the first place. Running into Darwish at the airport, drawing his attention. Realizing what he was up to.

Pronto sneezed. Her whole body shook, but she didn't roll upright.

Roxie smiled, turning to him. "I missed her, but thinking you were dead? I was completely lost."

"Not anymore, though," he said. "Not again. As much as it's in my control, you're not going to be alone. I'll always be here."

She nodded, sniffing away more tears. She looked exhausted. Wrung out and in need of some serious rest. They had to figure this out if they were going to end the threat, and in the middle of it all, he would have to make sure he and Roxie survived it long enough so they could heal.

Together, always.

Forever.

He leaned in to kiss her again—because he could and the team wasn't back yet. A second ambulance pulled up beside their SUV, close to the window beside Roxie. The driver honked the horn.

The ambulance they'd loaded Carim into revved and sped off, spinning the wheels and coughing up a bunch of smoke.

It tore off at top speed into traffic.

Moving way too fast.

FIVE

Roxie woke with a start, wrapped in blankets. Alone in a hotel room. Dim light. No one around her. "Liam!" She sat up, breathing hard.

A dream.

She couldn't have seen him. Rather, she must've hit her head and gone unconscious. Imagined the entire thing. He wasn't back. He was still dead, and she was wearing his shirt. Thinking of him. She must have—

The door to the right opened, and he rushed out. Roxie flinched. *Liam.*

"It's okay, it's okay." He wiped his mouth with a towel, the scent of mint on his breath when he gathered her into his arms.

Roxie held on. "I thought it was a dream."

Her dog scratched at the door, restless to get in.

Liam took her hand and set it on his chest, so she could feel the warmth of his skin and the beat of his heart. Roxie closed her eyes. *Thank You.* He was here, making it all the more tragic to think of losing a loved one and never being able to see them again. Even that split second that had made his return seem so much like a dream had been like torture. She couldn't even imagine.

"I'm okay."

He made a tiny noise in his throat. "No one expects that. I'm not okay. Look at me."

She opened her eyes. "You're not okay?"

He touched one hand to the side of his head, where he could almost hide the stitches by pulling his hair back. "I'm in one piece."

Roxie wasn't sure she could say the same about herself. She was still spinning out from the fact he wasn't dead. "How long am I going to feel like this?"

His expression softened from concern to something warmer and less like worry for her. "Not forever. It's okay, Rox. No one thinks anything of it. You reacted to what you knew. Now we have far more intel than we did before. I can keep going, but it'll sound like all I care about is the case."

"I know that's not true."

"Good. All I wanted was to get you back. Actually, I was worried I didn't care at *all* about the case." He shook his head, looking a little guilty. "But I found you, and you're good."

Pronto barked.

Liam got up, crossing to the door. "I should let her in."

Pronto raced between the smallest gap she could squeeze through and rushed over, hopping up on the bed. "Hey," Roxie said. "You know you're not supposed to be on furniture. Off."

Pronto turned and hopped off the bed, sitting beside it.

"She's hungry." Roxie pushed the covers back.

"I'll feed her." Liam went to the door. "You're okay?"

Roxie sighed. "I guess I will be at some point." She bit her lip. "Thank you for finding me."

Liam motioned to Pronto.

"You know what I mean."

He winked at her and went into the living room of their suite. Roxie rolled to the side, tangled in Liam's shirt and the blankets. She held out her hand, and Pronto set her muzzle in Roxie's palm. She rubbed her dog's fur. "Hey, girl."

Pronto licked her palm.

"I know. Me, too."

She'd been more than lost without Liam. Having Pronto gone also hadn't helped, and neither had her brother refusing to let her go get her dog. That whole situation was mixed up. Messed up. She needed even more time to process that, let alone to figure out how she was supposed to deal with thinking Liam was dead and then seeing him.

And the ambulance.

It had taken off right when a real ambulance showed up, speeding away with Carim inside. She'd been absorbed with Liam, but he was right. They needed to get to work on this insanity of a case.

Soon.

Any minute now.

Roxie flopped onto her back. In the other room, Pronto's food tumbled into her bowl. The dog scurried out, and Roxie heard the sink. He'd added water to her dry food. She closed her eyes, absorbing the feeling of having her family here. Of at least this small thing being right even if the rest of the world was in chaos and under the threat of a major disaster.

Don't let me ever take this for granted.

Liam came back to the door. "Gonna laze all day?"

She lifted her head.

"The team is on their way up. It's briefing time."

"Here?" She wasn't even dressed! Neither was Liam. The dog would need a walk to do some business it wasn't cool to accidently do on the carpet in a hotel room... Life's inevitable intrusion. The reprieve had been amazing.

He was right. It was time to get to work, to solve the case so they could carve out time and have another moment like this. Until one day, she realized they'd had a hundred more. Enough they'd spent so much time together they became complacent with it.

Liam had pulled on jeans and a T-shirt while she had her musings for a moment. Oops. "Coffee is brewing. It'll be a couple of minutes." He paused. "Are you gonna stare at me all day?"

"Probably."

His lips pulled up into a smile. "So lazy."

They both knew that wasn't what it was. Roxie shoved the covers back with a grunt and stomped to the shower. She gave it the three minute Marine Corps special and squeezed her hair dry with a towel. She came out of the bathroom in one of her shirts and a pair of jeans, looking for where she'd thrown the sweater she wanted to wear.

"Hey."

Roxie spun so fast she nearly fell over. "Dakota. Hey."

Her boss leaned against the bedroom door. "Can I come in? Or do you wanna take your dog outside, and I'll come with?"

"Let's do the potty run."

"There's a dog run in the corner of the parking lot on the grass berm. I'll bring Neema."

They leashed up the dogs, Roxie stuck her feet in her boots and kissed her husband. She didn't want to leave him, and he knew it because he winked at her. Outside was pretty empty, rows of cars but not many other signs of life. The hotel backed up to a hill, and she could hear traffic around the front.

"Doing okay?"

Roxie unclipped Pronto's leash and gave her the command to heel. Several times across the parking lot, she stopped for no reason. Pronto halted beside her. One time, she gave her dog the command to sit, another to lie down. Once they were at the dog run, she let Pronto go to play and have some fun being a dog for a while, not just a K-9.

"You are good at that." Dakota leaned against the fence, watching the dogs run and dance around each other. "But it's not the only reason I made the recommendation to hire you."

Roxie wasn't sure what to make of that. "You didn't just hire me, you hired Liam and me together. Pronto was an add on."

"You took a starting point, ran with it, and made it into something impressive."

"And never got the chance to even get it off the ground."

Dakota said, "That would be true if your husband weren't alive. But I want to say this, and you need to hear me well. Even without Liam, I'd still want you on the team. With or without Pronto, in fact. Whether or not you were a US Marshal. All those are just added bonuses."

"What exactly would I bring to the table with no partner, no K-9, and no badge?"

"*You*." Dakota said, "That's what I need you to get."

Roxie started to shake her head.

"Girl, that is *exactly* what I'm talking about. You have a role here, and you're the only one who can do it. That's what I need you to understand."

"Because I didn't call?"

Dakota watched the dogs. "You could have."

If she'd pushed it with her brother, Roxie wasn't sure what would have happened. But she doubted they'd have kept her from a phone if she'd been desperate and adamant.

"You don't trust us."

Roxie started to argue, but Dakota held up a hand.

She continued, "That's my problem to fix, not yours. You're as much a part of this team as any of us, and we work until you believe it. That's what makes this team a family." Dakota paused, and Roxie felt the warmth of that focused attention on her. "That's what I had to learn, and now I get to prove it to you."

"I want to help bring Darwish in."

"You're more like me than you realize." Dakota chuckled. "Liam will want to be there, too. We need to ensure he doesn't push it too hard. He took a hit in that explosion."

"I knew he wasn't all right!" He'd been moving slowly, but the rush of having him back, she'd overlooked the slight slur in his speech when he got tired right before he'd taken that nap. "Should he be in the hospital?"

"I'll get his mom on the phone. She can explain what the doctor said."

Roxie swallowed. "Liam's mom?"

"That's what I said." Dakota eyed her.

She winced. "What is she going to say?"

"Doesn't matter," Dakota said. "You're gonna listen. You're gonna say thank you, and then you're gonna promise you'll take care of her son."

Was Olivia O'Connell going to blame Roxie for what happened to him? Or would she blame her for not being there when he woke up? Roxie let go of the bite on her lip.

"You're gonna face down a dangerous foreign warlord, and you're scared of Liam's mother?"

Roxie shot Dakota a look, which made her laugh.

"I wouldn't know. Josh and I don't have in-laws to worry about. Just nosy friends."

Roxie wanted to talk about the investigation now. "Liam's mother has been nothing but nice to me."

"And you have no idea how to deal with it?"

Roxie shrugged. "Let's get back inside."

Dakota nodded, and they both called their dogs. As they went back to the rear door, she noticed Dakota scanning. Protecting Roxie. Maybe watching for Darwish—or whoever he'd sent to take her out. Or Adam and his men, who'd disappeared.

Roxie didn't want to be the vulnerable, protected one. She wanted to get this done so she could be an equal team member. Dakota was right that she hadn't felt confident in her own abilities. She'd been along for the ride, even as a Marshal. Could she really have a place that felt like equal standing with the others?

I want that, Lord. Is that what You are doing? It seemed like He wanted to pour out yet more blessings. Not leave her the way she was but build her up so she could do amazing things. It was hard to believe, but even that was something to have confidence in.

Back upstairs in the room, everyone had gathered around, standing or sitting with coffee mugs in their hands.

Roxie let Pronto off her leash, and Liam wrapped his arms around her. "Good?"

She looked up at him, sliding her hands up his arms. "I am now."

Someone made a gagging sound. She ignored Niall and his, "Are they going to quit this?"

Liam kissed her on the nose. "Work time."

"Darn."

Dakota chuckled. "Coffee first. Everything else after."

"I knew there was a reason I liked you." She accepted the mug from her boss. "Thanks."

"You're welcome. Ready to run down your brother's team for us? Then we'll get into the disappearing ambulance and the search for Darwish."

Roxie braced herself but realized she didn't have to worry.

This was her team.

"Right." Roxie took a swig of fortifying coffee. "Adam."

SIX

Liam wanted to hang onto Roxie and not let go. Too bad the team briefing wasn't really the place to do that. He stood over by the breakfast bar style counter, where Talia sat with her laptop. Roxie stood close, holding her coffee with two hands.

Whatever Dakota had said to her while they'd taken the dogs outside seemed to have helped her settle at least some. He liked this team and wanted her to feel like she had a support system. His heart felt like it was breaking in his chest just thinking about her reaction to the fact she'd been told he was dead.

He wanted to throttle whoever told her that. And she'd believed it.

She'd spun out, reeling, and shut everyone and everything out. He needed her to know she had people who would help her through something like that.

Her brother certainly hadn't.

He wanted to throttle that guy as well. She'd been in pain and raging silently, but had her brother taken care of her? No. He'd put her at risk and had her working. As soon as her actual family showed up, he split and went back to his job.

If they met again, Liam had some things to say to Adam Helton.

"Careful there, kid."

He realized Talia was talking to him.

"Deep breaths."

Liam focused on what Dakota was saying, something about the three vans that had been rented. The cabin where they'd been chased by Adam and his team for whatever reason—because they'd been trying to "rescue" Roxie from him? He didn't know, and his head hurt too much to figure it out right now.

He probably needed another pain pill.

"...nothing."

Liam blew out a breath and drank some more coffee, needing mundane things to center himself in the here and now and focus his thoughts.

Everyone looked at Roxie.

Liam shifted slightly closer to her, so the outside of their arms were touching. Giving her a semblance of solidarity she needed to anchor her. *She needs to know this team will support her.* Liam prayed silently, asking for help to figure out how to convince her of what she had in front of her. Not just him but the whole taskforce and the way he knew they could be.

A family.

Not just work friends she was close with, but also his family who would happily claim her as their own.

Roxie said, "They seem to operate from a boat. The *Vanguard* which makes sense, as their team operates under my former employer. Though, it seems like their whole operation is off book. I had never heard of them."

Dakota sat forward in her chair. "Any idea how to find them?"

He figured Roxie wanted to ask, so he said, "Why do you need to get in touch with them? Or is this about shutting them down?" Just so her asking didn't seem like her loyalties were divided.

Sometimes it seemed like Dakota was three steps ahead of everyone else's thought process. Maybe that was boss's prerogative, but he also thought it might be how she calculated things in her mind.

Dakota glanced at Josh, who nodded. "Three days ago, a plane registered to a Silicon Valley company blew up minutes after takeoff from a tiny regional airport. On board were two pilots, three company employees, the CEO of an international bank—our Chinese banker—and a state senator. No one thought anything of them being together."

Niall said, "But now they're all dead, and people are asking questions online. Why they were all in that company plane when they shouldn't have overlapping interests that the public isn't cognizant of. Why they were meeting, traveling together, and who wanted to kill them."

Liam frowned. "Any sense there was mechanical failure that led to the crash?"

Dakota shook her head. "Very clearly an explosive device. No one found it during pre-flight checks, which means negligence. But this was thought out and planned."

"And the internet is spinning out as to why."

She nodded. "One of our working theories is that this is the second of three incidents, the first being the train explosion you were both in. The third possibly having to do with a boat, given the emojis on those texts you found."

Roxie inhaled sharply. "And you think my brother's boat might be the next target?"

"It's certainly possible." Niall glanced around.

"What about the master plan?" Liam asked.

Dakota tipped her head to the side. "That's where things get more abstract. It could fit into the endgame Carim came up with, or Darwish could be riffing off that plan and elaborating on it to come up with his own."

Roxie said, "Where do these smaller incidents fit in?"

Liam was glad she asked. He wanted to know as well, but there was so much going on in his head right now. Her. His marriage. How they were going to settle long enough to sort through some of these things and find a little peace. Meanwhile, they seemed to have hit the ground running on caseload, and it looked like life as a federal agent didn't usually slow down.

He was going to have to be careful to make sure they had a life/work balance.

Dakota said, "The plane crash fits in with the overall plan of destabilizing the economy, state and federal, and has the FBI and a lot of other resources working on shutting down what looks, on the surface, like a plan to do just that. Meanwhile, their response times on anything else are delayed, since it means diverting resources and splitting their focus."

"So, it's basically misdirection?" Roxie took a sip of her coffee. "Sounds like something Adam would come up with."

Liam thought it sounded like a stretch. An elaborate plan that might even be overly so. In local law enforcement, he'd discovered that the simplest answer usually was the one that turned out to be the truth. A lot of people who wanted to cause mass chaos did so for some ideological reason, not just because they could and it proved their power.

"We should warn him." Roxie reached into her pocket and pulled out a business card with a phone number on it...and one the other side the letters VR.

Talia reached over in front of Liam, her hand out to Roxie. "May I?"

Roxie hesitated enough to show that she was clearly warring with indecision. She set the card in Talia's hand. "Thanks, T."

"We'll keep him safe, girl. You know that."

Roxie might not, but he figured she was learning. Liam said, "What's next?"

Dakota nodded. "Assignments are in your email. Niall is visiting the nearest port, and he'll talk with the local NCIS office about the possibility of a threat. Josh and I are going to follow up on a lead with the ambulance and try to nail down where Darwish took his brother."

Liam still couldn't believe the man had shot his own brother just so he could intercept with an ambulance and "rescue" Carim.

Did Adam and his team know how thoroughly they'd been duped?

The taskforce had found information about the exchange that should have gone down in that city park. Plus information as to the hit out on both him and Roxie.

Darwish was gunning for them.

"What are Roxie and I doing?" Sure, he could read his email, but he wanted to be certain Dakota had heard him that he would be with Roxie, and they weren't going to get separated. The taskforce was an odd mix of couples, partners, and friends. They made it work, sometimes together and sometimes in friendly competition with each other.

This, however, wasn't up for discussion.

Unless she pushed it as his boss and put her foot down. But Liam couldn't see anyone doing that after the last two weeks Roxie and Liam had been through.

Dakota gave him a look like, *calm down.* "The two of you have a meeting in thirty minutes with a scientist at the local college. I haven't been able to get ahold of her, but the school said she should be coming in for class shortly. An expert in geography and environmental science. She's going to talk to you about the likely places Darwish would have to plant bombs in order for them to be effective on the scale outlined in Carim's master plan."

"Got it." They didn't have much time to waste if they were going to make that meeting.

"I'll stay here...in *my* room or the conference room." Talia lifted her laptop and slid her gold purse over her shoulder. "Call if you need tech support." She nudged Roxie's shoulder on the way past. "Good to have you back."

The rest of them shook hands and made plans to reconnect later for dinner so they could debrief. As far as he could tell, the threat was imminent, but since they had no idea what timeframe Darwish was working on, his guess was as good as anyone's.

Roxie held his hand down to the car, the dog

leash in her other. Surrounded by family. Did she realize that?

Liam waited while she loaded Pronto into her crate in the back and then held her door for her. She paused, looking up at him, then lifted up and kissed his cheek. "Love you."

Soaking it in. Absorbing what she had back. What she'd never lost, not really, even though to her it probably felt like she had.

He should call his mom and tell her that Roxie was back with him, but then he'd have to explain that she hadn't been truly kidnapped. He sent a quick text telling her all was well and that he'd tell her the whole story later.

His phone beeped as he buckled up. "Mom says she loves us both, and we should take care."

Roxie smiled gently at him, warm and soft but also unsure.

"What is it?"

"Later...we should talk again about the wedding."

Not what he'd thought she would be thinking about. She didn't need a bucketload of pressure after that gentle declaration. He held her hand, leaned over and gave her a soft kiss. "Sounds good."

Liam felt better than he had since he woke up in the hospital as he drove over to the local state college. He found the right building, and they explained to the college student behind the dark wood welcome desk who they were and the fact they had an appointment.

Having the same last name would probably always get them an odd look, the same way everyone they met would want to know what kind of dog Pronto was and what she could do. Liam didn't want it any other way. Roxie belonged to his family as much as he did, as far as he was concerned. She wanted to claim that association by using his last name.

It was just a matter of convincing her heart.

The walls were lined with the same wood wainscoting as the welcome desk, giving the whole building a very old-world, or East Coast, feel. A place of higher learning that could charge more because they looked like they knew what they were doing. He'd gone to community college on the GI bill, so he didn't really get it.

Muted talking came from somewhere. As well as the smell of books, which his mom claimed was superior to any scent.

"I think this is it." Roxie pointed to the name plate beside the door, indicating this was the office of Sierra Hapworth, PhD. She knocked on the frosted glass, but no one answered, which was odd considering the fact she should be here to prep for her class. Had Dakota made a mistake with the time?

"Didn't she say the professor was in here?" Liam nudged down the handle, all his instincts waking up.

The door wasn't locked.

Pronto sniffed at the inch wide opening and shook her head.

"I have no idea what that alert means," Roxie said. "But it's not good."

SEVEN

Up until the door opened and Pronto alerted like that, Roxie had been enjoying the fact Liam had seemed receptive about the wedding. Or at least about the idea of one being back on the table. She'd been thinking about their future when she should be thinking about the case.

Lives were at stake.

She clicked her tongue. Pronto stilled, her body tight. Roxie unclipped her leash and gave her enough of an opening in the door. She gave Pronto the command to clear a room, which meant flushing out any bad guys that might be hiding.

Sure, it put her dog at risk if there was someone threatening hiding in the office, but Roxie entered right behind her. Weapon drawn. Soft footsteps. Pronto disappeared into an inner office, and a few seconds later came out. She set her doggie butt on the carpet, eyes alert. Ears pricked for any disturbances.

"Good girl." Roxie touched the tight muscle on Pronto's shoulder and patted twice. She stepped into the office, knowing the K-9 would stand guard at the door. Roxie got a look at what Pronto had found. "Oh."

"What is it?" Liam touched the small of her back. "Room looks clear other than...oh. I'll call it in."

"Good idea." She rounded the desk. Not the first dead body she'd ever seen. Roxie only got close enough to touch two fingers to the neck of the woman sitting in her office chair with the high back. *Yep, no pulse.* The woman's hands were tied to the arms of the chair, blood dripping from her mouth. What looked like multiple stab wounds peppered her torso and abdomen. "She's dead, and it might've been hours ago because she's cold."

Liam nodded, relaying the information to whoever was on the other end of the phone. "Thanks." He hung up. "Quick look around without leaving trace evidence, and then we're in the hallway when they get here."

If he wanted her to look around thoroughly, he should've given her more time than that.

The corner of Liam's mouth curled up. "Clock's ticking."

She got to work, looking at the papers on the desk. She used a pen to nudge the mouse so the computer monitor woke up. "She was looking at a map. Looks like a mountain range and a mine."

Roxie took a photo of the screen with her phone so she could send it to Talia.

"They wanted information."

Roxie went to the far side of the desk. "Because she was tortured?" The idea of it wasn't something that sat right in her stomach. "I want to know why no one heard it."

"Could be this happened in the pre-dawn hours

when no one was here, and no one has been in here this morning."

Roxie didn't like the idea of someone being dead for hours before they were even discovered. Someone should've noticed. A loved one should have realized she was missing and tried to find her.

Did anyone even care?

"Hey." Liam spoke softly. He touched her waist. "Step outside with me."

"I'll take Pronto outside for some air." She wanted Liam to come with her because the idea of being apart was about as much of a nice feeling as that nightmare she'd had where this was all a dream. But they couldn't leave the crime scene.

"I'll be out there as soon as someone gets here." He squeezed her waist gently, and she clipped Pronto's leash back on.

Her footsteps echoed in the hall, along with Pronto's nails—which meant she needed them cut. Roxie glanced over her shoulder and saw Liam watching them leave. As she stepped outside onto the wide stone steps in front of the humanities building, trying to appreciate the warmth of the sun, she spotted her brother to one side, talking to one of his men. Roxie made a beeline for him. "Did you kill her?"

Of course Pronto noted her tension and switched to high alert.

He had the decency to flinch at least. "You really think I'd stick around if I had?"

He wasn't going to say he hadn't, just that he wouldn't still be here. "Did you go in the professor's office?"

"Don't worry. You won't find my DNA in there."

Roxie's K-9 sniffed the knees of her brother's

pants, then his boots. Only when Pronto had his scent did he hold out his fist for sniffs. After that, he gave chin scratches.

At which point, her ferocious working dog pretty much turned into a pile of goo with a crush on the tough guy. Roxie frowned. "Why can't you just tell me you didn't kill her?"

Adam lifted his chin. "Would you even believe me? What else has that husband of yours been filling your head with?"

"Liam isn't the enemy here." His presence in her life was everything good she had. The evidence she'd found of a good God who gave His children good things. Without Liam, she wouldn't even believe in Him.

At least that was what she had right now. Roxie hoped that one day her faith wasn't so fragile, and that she could build more and more to be able to stand firm even with nothing.

"No? I saw the way he shoved you on that hilltop."

When Liam had told her to run. "He was going to face all of you. Alone. He was defending me. Giving me the chance to escape."

She lifted her chin, probably the same expression on her face that he had. She and Adam weren't all that dissimilar. Roxie figured in time, she'd have become a lot more like him. If it wasn't for the fact that Liam hadn't been dead.

She said, "What happened at the park? Your guys had a shooter on the roof, and then you left. Did they get away?"

"It was misdirection. The man who shot Carim was on the ground. We took down the rooftop shooter, and the man who chased the ground level shooter caught his man, too. Both are lower level. Local guys hired for the day."

"Like the ones who burned down the cabin." She frowned. "Although, to be honest, I did think that was you guys—or friends of yours."

Adam huffed. "As if."

For a split second, he almost looked like the teen she'd known. Watching it was a different kind of grief, knowing who he had been and the man she'd just spent a week with. Or perhaps her heart hadn't quite let go of the sorrow even though Liam was back.

Roxie spoke softly. "One day, you should tell me what happened to you."

"You don't need to know." He shook his head, his face plain in a way she didn't like. He was about to say something else but turned abruptly to face away from her.

Roxie caught what he'd seen and watched two uniformed police officers jog down the path that cut across the courtyard and into the building.

Hiding his identity. Living his life below the radar.

Adam turned back to her as soon as the "threat" had passed. "Once this case is over, you'll probably never see me again."

Roxie's chest clenched like steel bands, the feel of being trapped with no way out. "I'm supposed to be okay with that? You hide from the police. So...what? You can't see me because I'm a cop?"

Her mind didn't want to contend with the idea she'd become a Marshal to be closer to Liam, and it was family that might make her consider throwing it all away. Liam would win—always. But that didn't mean a good part of her didn't want to have her brother in her life if she could.

It had never been an option before.

"It's not because you're a cop." His expression softened, but it didn't relieve any of the hard edges. "I'm so proud of you." He reacted again, shifting. This time, it was Liam's proximity.

Roxie held out her hand, and her husband came over, linking his fingers with hers.

Liam's entire focus seemed to be on her brother, though. "We good? Or do you need to threaten me one more time so you can be confident you got your point across?"

Her brother almost smiled. Then he looked at Roxie. "Tell your taskforce people I'm good. I don't need a warning to keep my stuff tight. I can protect what's mine."

In his own way, she figured that's what he thought he was doing with her. "The next explosion is supposed to be a boat."

"I'm good." Adam shifted his stance, like he wanted to walk away, but there was more to say. "Don't worry about me, Rox."

He gave Pronto point-two seconds of chin scratches and left.

Liam squeezed her hand, just enough to get her attention. When she turned to him, the breeze fluttered some hair across her face.

She swiped it back and tucked it behind her ear.

Pronto whined.

Roxie shook her head. "I think she's in love with my brother."

Liam snorted. He looked like wanted to ask her if

she was all right but thankfully kept the question to himself. "Cops have the scene here."

Her phone chimed in her pocket. Roxie checked the screen. "I got an email from Simon."

"Anything we need?"

"I haven't talked to him or Peter since..."

Liam nodded. "Cops have the scene. We can go, but we need to get them statements today."

She thumbed open the email. "Huh. PDFs but they have Vanguard encryption. I'll need access to a computer to look at the files, assuming my password is still good."

They started toward the car. "Any idea what it is?"

She read the body of the email. It was past time to call and let the twins know she was all right. "They miss me. They hope I'm all right. Simon said this is the IDs for the two shooters at the park, a full workup of who they are, and statements of what they told Adam's team. They've been turned over to the local police precinct with all the evidence including video footage."

"Great. We can take a look," Liam said. "It could yield something on Darwish and where he took Carim."

She replied to Simon's email with the image she had taken of the dead professor's computer screen. Simply in the interest of exchanging information. "What I want to know is what the murderer wanted from the professor. The information was worth killing her over, evidently."

Liam held the car door open for her. "Knowledge of where to put the bombs for maximum effectiveness? That's why we came."

Roxie stood between the door and the car. "Maybe that's what they wanted, but she could've been working with Darwish, and maybe they didn't like when she withheld information."

It wasn't such a stretch for someone like the guys on Adam's team to be the ones to want information from the professor. If they hadn't killed her, which she was glad of, then it had to be that she'd stood up against the bad guy they were looking for, and he'd sent someone to kill her. After they found out everything she knew.

Roxie slid into the seat, and he closed the door. By the time he'd rounded the car and got in, she had a reply from Simon. "Whoa."

"What is it?"

"Well, now at least I know why my brother was standing there." She shook her head. "He was getting Simon access to the network, probably through his proximity to the computers. Even from outside the building. And Simon used it to piggyback his way into their system. He sent me the contents of the professor's hard drive."

Once they got to her computer, she'd be able to use her password and dig into the information, but in the email, he explained enough to know the wealth of what Vanguard—thanks to her brother being here— had obtained.

She glanced over at Liam. "We now have a better idea where the bombs might be."

EIGHT

The only thing Liam needed help with when it came to Roxie was walking her down the aisle. He certainly didn't need her brother hanging around with his rough looking teammates when it came to keeping her safe. He much preferred the idea that Adam had been there working, gathering his own intel. If the guy wanted to hang around, then he'd get a clue pretty fast that Liam could protect his wife.

He even had a K-9 to help.

Roxie crumpled up the wrapper to her tacos and stuffed it in the bag where he'd put the wrapper that came with his burrito. "Tortilla chips?"

He held onto the steering wheel with one hand and turned the volume slightly up on the radio. "I'm stuffed."

She folded the top over on the bag and set it by her feet, lifting her paper cup and sipping from the straw.

The light turned green, and Liam hit the gas, pulling onto the on-ramp for the freeway. Fifty feet later, the traffic meter tempered the flow of vehicles.

Liam let off the gas since it was red, then when the light turned green, he sped up.

"Pretty sure the mountain will still be there when we get there. It's not going anywhere."

They were heading to the closest spot on the map the professor had left on her computer. Still, he got the feeling they were running up against the clock. "I don't like the idea that they're ahead of us. We're playing catch up, and there are so many lives at stake."

"It is scary." She set her drink in the cupholder. "Did you even know the taskforce did this stuff?"

"I didn't know they existed." He shot her a smile.

"Kind of like my brother and his team," she said. "This whole world that civilians never even know about. Like the number of terror plots or deadly crimes the police stop, saving everyone from what would've been the worst day of their lives."

He nodded. "So, let's talk about something good instead while we wait for the team to call us back." He wondered if they would do this often on cases where they were partnered up. While Pronto snored in the back of the car. "Why don't you have Simon and Peter walk you down the aisle? Since you guys are good friends."

Roxie shifted, a jerky move he didn't understand. "What?"

"You want to talk about that right now?"

He shrugged. "I don't know. Do I?"

Roxie rolled her eyes. Yeah, he was such a guy. "We haven't even decided if we're going to spend money on a wedding celebration, let alone that there will be an aisle to walk down."

"You wanna just have a party? That's fine by me."

"Is that all you want?"

Liam said, "I want what you want."

"That's the worst answer ever."

"Even if it's the truth?"

Roxie sighed. "Yes, I suppose it wouldn't be awful to have my friends walk me down the aisle. Except that we already got married. I also suppose I could ask Bob Davis, since he's a friend, too. And a friend of your family."

Liam winced. "More than a friend apparently. My mother told me it's pretty serious."

"Maybe they'll be the ones getting married."

Liam's foot slipped off the gas.

"She might need *you* to walk her down the aisle."

His mind eclipsed. The dash display shifted to show an incoming call, and the sound came through the car speakers. "That's terrifying." He tapped the screen. "O'Connell."

"And O'Connell."

The caller said, "You guys sound like a law firm."

Roxie chuckled. "I didn't realize. But you're right, T. We kind of do."

Talia said, "Okay, we've split up and we're checking out the locations indicated by the professor, so that's all in process. Updates when you have them. As for me, I got footage from the college security system during the time of the professor's murder. Which, from the time he entered and the time he left, took approximately fifty-two minutes to complete."

Roxie said, "Yeesh."

Liam had seen people tortured before, and this one hadn't been on the horrifying end of the scale. But it had been bad enough, and a woman was dead.

"I'm sending over an image of him now. Tell me if

you recognize him at all. It's a longshot, but the two of you have met more of the players in this since you got there."

Roxie's phone buzzed.

Liam changed lanes, driving at top speed on the freeway but not ready yet to add his lights and siren.

He heard her breathy inhale. "I know him."

Liam glanced over but couldn't look without causing a traffic accident. "Who is he? One of Adam's guys?" She'd have said if it had been her brother in the footage.

"Do you have a name for me?"

Roxie said, "No, sorry. He was at the compound, part of the group who were breaking out Carim. I thought Adam and his team killed all of these guys, but this one must have survived."

"I'll be sure to email Vanguard and explain their team allowed something critical to slip through the cracks." Talia let out a little satisfied chuckle. "No idea what his name might be?"

"No," Roxie said. "Sorry."

"No worries. Thanks, guys."

Liam said, "Keep in touch."

"You know it." The line went dead.

"Are you going to ask me about weddings some more?"

Liam wanted to, but instead said, "Tell me about this mountain we're looking at. Any idea why the professor pinpointed it?" He changed lanes since their exit was coming up.

Roxie looked at her phone. "From what she's got here, in her report that she put together..."

"Is there a name on that? Who she did it for?"

"No, but Simon is looking into it. Now that we

know one of Darwish's mercenaries killed her, maybe it was because he's on the outs, and he wanted back in. Darwish could've sent him, but if he failed at the compound getting Carim out, then maybe he's trying to get back in the boss's good graces."

"Now you're thinking like a cop." Liam took the exit and found signs for a lookout. The directions Talia had sent them had him pull off before that, onto a dirt track with No Trespassing signs. "Looks like this place has been shut down for a while."

Trees crowded the road, barely a dirt track carved out of the side of the hill. He drove the winding curves between a steep drop off and the incline above them to the right. If anyone came the other direction, he'd have to figure out where to pull off, and there would still be barely any space with two cars and the edge where a descent to death waited.

Liam spotted a squirrel race down a tree and across the road.

Two bends and most of the mountain height later, they leveled off at a clearing where someone had parked a van with a satellite dish on the roof.

Roxie said, "Not the kind of vehicle you'd think to see up here."

"Neither is the one we're driving, but we should check it out." He pulled over on the opposite end of the clearing, parking so Roxie was protected on the far side of the car. "You grab Pronto, and we can walk around."

"Copy that." She shoved her door open.

He got out and looked around, spotting the entrance to a cave—or a mine—beyond the van between the trees. Not the main entrance to anything that would've been set up as a business at any point. If it was part of a larger network, this was maybe a back way in and out.

Maybe part of a historical mining operation.

"This is it?" Roxie strode over, Pronto beside her.

"Looks like it." He didn't set off yet, though. "This is recon only. We're just going to have a look and see who is here and what they're doing."

Roxie gave him a short nod. "Sounds like a plan."

They cleared the van, and then Liam went first, over to the entrance to the mine. He spotted multiple sets of footprints, sunk deep into the ground. "Looks like at least two or three people, and they were carrying something heavy, maybe?"

"From the prints?"

Liam nodded, close to the entrance of what looked like a cave. How deep did it go? "They're so deep it has to be weight-related. So, either they're big guys, like abnormally large, because look at mine in comparison." His boots weren't sinking that far into the mud. "Or they were carrying heavy things."

"Like a bomb." She sounded as nervous as her expression looked.

"Just recon."

"Got it."

They stepped inside, out of the daylight into the cave which turned out to be more of a tunnel. Not big enough for the kind of truck a mining operation might use, but a person could probably drive a small pickup down here.

Every fifteen or so feet, a lantern had been anchored into the ceiling, providing just enough light they could see where they were going. Pronto made almost no sound, at least compared to his and Roxie's footsteps.

Dirt rained down, and once in a while, a lantern swayed.

As they approached the end, where light glowed brighter, he had to add this to the mental list he had going of things he'd never expected would happen. Not when they were supposed to be on vacation and definitely not working.

When this was done, they were going to need a vacation from their vacation.

He paused before the end, listening first before he ever stepped out. Liam leaned out instead, peering into the space where three men stood around a crate. He palmed his gun before he even realized what his reaction should be. *Recon.* They could head back out, call this in, and get local police or a sheriff's department cop to meet them. Spend some time questioning these guys to find out who they were and what they were doing here.

Roxie shifted slightly behind him, and he heard the metal snick of her unclipping Pronto's leash. He heard her gun slide out of the holster. She was ready for anything that might go down now.

Liam wished he could send her out and take care of this solo, but that was never what their relationship had been. Maybe when they started having kids, things would change and instead of just wanting to protect her, he would be able to go out knowing she was safe and so were any children they had.

The men in the open room continued to talk. It got heated, and one shoved another.

Beyond them, the third man with the crate between him and everything else zeroed his gaze in on the entrance where he and Roxie stood. *Busted.* Liam started to back up, about to tell Roxie to run.

A bullet pinged off the dirt wall beside his head.

No way. Liam said, "Split. Pronto." He ducked right, moving into the room, already firing. Pronto raced over to the men and slammed into one, full speed, taking the man down.

Roxie yelled a command and went left. She ran to the guy on her side.

Liam squeezed off two shots in the direction of the third man, now crouching behind the crate. He ran to the guy with Pronto on top of him, her powerful jaw locked on his arm. The man screamed and batted at the dog, trying to get away.

"Pronto," Liam ordered, "Out."

The dog let go of the guy and backed up. Liam held his gun trained on the man. "Hands where I can see them."

Behind him Roxie grunted like she'd been punched in the stomach. A gun discharged. For one heartbeat, he knew how she'd felt hearing he was dead, and then he heard a male yelp. The sound of a person hitting the ground.

The man on the floor in front of him flinched.

Number three shifted. "It's done. Go. Go."

Liam started to turn. The guy from the ground launched up and clipped his shoulder, rushing past Liam. Roxie hit the ground hard, and the man who'd been by the crate sprinted past her to the entrance.

Pronto ran to her. Liam went around the crate and gaped at what he found there. "Not good."

"What is it?" Roxie asked.

"Whatever this device is? It's armed."

NINE

Why did her life feel right, in the middle of something so wrong? Roxie didn't have time to ponder the mysteries of why fighting side by side with Liam had to feel so right when she was also staring at a nuclear warhead.

She told Pronto to lie down and raced over to look.

The LED screen had a single red light, circling around the sides of the square display. "It's counting down." And each circuit of the screen meant...what? "How much time do we have?"

Liam touched her side, and she gave herself a second to feel his reassuring strength. She tucked her elbow in, holding his hand there on her ribs. Just a moment, but it was all she needed.

"We have to get out of here."

"But we can't let it go off. We wouldn't be able to run far enough, fast enough, to get clear. And without everyone within hundreds of miles doing the same thing, there would be far too many casualties.

"So, we should die with them because we can't

stop it?" Roxie gasped. "There's no way to tell how long we have. It could be hours."

"I doubt it. They left in a hurry." Liam pulled out his phone. "I'll call Talia."

She did the same. "Adam. Maybe one of his guys knows how to shut this thing off."

"We have to do what we can, even if it doesn't work. We have to try."

Roxie figured they would die trying.

She crouched, looking at the warhead, while she held the phone to her ear and listened to it ring. When the ringing stopped, she hung up and dialed again.

A couple of rings in, he picked up. "I'm kind of busy right—"

"Does anyone on your team know how to disarm a nuclear warhead?"

"Roxie, what did you—"

"Just tell me!"

She heard a shuffle on his end. "Ash, call Sie. Get him on the line. I need a location on Roxie's phone. We're moving. *Now*. Drop everything and get to the car." He barely took a breath and said, "Ice, take the phone. Tell her how to disarm."

Roxie could have fainted with relief. She looked at Liam, walking while he talked to Talia. When he glanced over, she said, "Adam has a guy."

Liam nodded, a whole lot of longing in his expression. She knew exactly how he felt. She had him back, and now this might be the end. For them, and for a lot of other people.

Lord, help us.

"Tell me what you have." The gruff voice jogged

her out of her prayer. "Better yet, turn on your video and show me."

"Okay." Roxie tapped the screen and then flipped the camera. "He said he armed it, and then they all ran off. Is it gonna kill us all?"

She didn't really want to ask, and the sick feeling in her stomach wasn't going anywhere anytime soon.

"That isn't how nukes work. But it will explode if we don't do something." Ice studied the screen, looking for small details. She backed up so he could see the whole thing. He said, "Show me the panel."

She moved in and listened to Liam hang up with Talia.

"Step to the right."

As soon as she did, Ice muttered something. "This isn't good, Nix."

Adam moved into view on the screen, over his shoulder. "Nothing you haven't done before." His tone made it sound like this was no big deal, but she saw what Ice didn't. The look in his eyes indicated Adam knew this was a *very* big deal.

Roxie's hand shook. She steadied it with the other holding the phone. "Someone tell me what to do before this nuke blows up in all of our faces." Everyone she cared about in the world would be caught in the blast.

Pronto broke her *down* and came over. Roxie couldn't even be mad when the dog was reacting to her demeanor, feeling Roxie's stress, and wanted to do something to help her. Comfort her.

The K-9 leaned against her leg, and Roxie leaned right back.

"We need to dismantle. We won't be able to disarm it, not the way this was built."

Roxie said, "Just tell me how to turn it off!"

"Can't do that, kid." Ice was mid-thirties, but she accepted the endearment. It wasn't like there was time to argue. "Tell me what you've got. A screwdriver, prybar, hammer? What are we working with?"

Roxie spun around, left then right. "I have nothing."

She wasn't going to shoot at it!

Liam moved to her side, flicking his hand. "I have a multitool. What are we doing?" His face was all business, but the way he stood by her signaled that protective instinct she knew ran deep. He didn't want to be here any more than she did.

Or maybe it was more that he didn't want *her* anywhere near this.

"Two screws," Ice said. "Top left and top right. Remove the panel. Carefully."

"We're going to get radiation poisoning," Roxie muttered.

Liam got to work on the screws. "Why don't you ask him how he knows this stuff?"

"Because there's no time to chat!" She wasn't being a hysterical female, even though they were both looking at her like she was. If there was a time to freak out, then *this* was the time to freak out.

Liam's lips twitched. "I don't want to be here. I don't want you here. But we are."

"So we deal?"

"We're either gonna die, or we're gonna fix this and everyone gets to live today."

Roxie said, "I know which one I'm choosing." She didn't want to tell him to hurry up. He was already going faster than she would be able to, and being impatient could distract him.

Ice looked behind him. "Yeah, the bigger case. That thing is at least three feet long." He nodded, then stood, moving through halls.

She couldn't tell where he was, but he stepped through a door that took him outside. A few more steps, and he climbed into a vehicle.

"Got it." Liam's two discarded screws enabled him to pop the panel and remove it. "What next?"

Roxie's stomach lurched. "This is insane." She pointed the phone at the panel and showed her brother's teammate the inner workings.

"Okay, now we're getting somewhere." Ice peered at the screen. "I know who made this. Or at least who designed it." He swore aloud, and Roxie winced.

She said, "We just cut a wire, and we're good, right?" She was ready to be done with this. *Now*.

"You're gonna have to take the whole detonator out. After that, the radioactive material will be inert. This kind of bomb, one smaller piece of plutonium is fired into a bigger disk, and it's the collision that creates the explosion."

"Like a bullet fired at a plate." Liam peered at it. "And it's the pieces of the plate that cause destruction, flying out in every direction."

"Correct." Ice said, "You're going to reach in, grab those two arms coming out either side of the center circle part, and pull up. We need to see how it's connected so just go far enough that we can get a look under it."

Liam wiped his hands on his jeans, then reached for it. He paused and turned to her. "I love you so much."

A lump rose in Roxie's throat.

"I want to give you everything. I wish we had long enough I could."

Roxie swallowed, shaking her head. "I don't need anything."

He looked a little sad at that. "I was gonna fix that, too."

Then he turned to the device and lifted the two arms between his index finger and thumb on each hand and got it up a couple of inches so they could see underneath.

He was going to fix her? Or fix what she thought? Roxie's mind didn't want to focus on anything but what Liam had just said.

She managed to make sure the phone had a view of what they needed to see. Inside, however, she couldn't stop thinking about it. He had to know she only needed him. She was right where she'd always wanted to be—except for the restless dog and the nuclear bomb that could explode at any moment.

Roxie didn't have much, but that meant she didn't need much.

She was working out how to rely on God. How to live, grateful for what she had—which was a lot when she listed it all. Liam. Her job. Pronto. Their life.

Why would she need anything else?

Liam obviously didn't agree, or he wouldn't want to change it. Change *her*. She had no idea what to think about it. She just knew it was better if she didn't get mad at him.

"Pull hard, just pull it out."

Liam wasted no time complying with Ice's order. He whipped the detonator back, and wires snapped.

The panel on the front went dark. "Does that mean it's disarmed?"

"Why make it hard? It's not like these guys are rocket scientists."

"No," Roxie said, "but they are nuclear physicists."

Ice laughed. "I knew you were good people."

"Can we get this thing out of here—?"

Her question was cut off by Liam grasping her elbow and spinning her to him. She yelped and slammed into him. Liam pressed a hard kiss on her lips that wasn't entirely comfortable, but she understood what he was feeling.

She clung to him for a second, reveling in the feel of being alive even if she wound up with bruised lips and the need to catch her breath. There was a time for sweet and a time for desperate, and life was full of all the in-betweens.

"You guys wanna get going?" Ice sounded far away.

Liam pulled back, smiling.

She frowned. "We should talk."

"Uh-oh." Ice chuckled. "Someone's in trouble."

Roxie looked at the phone. "Tell us where to take this detonator so I can hang up."

"No need. We're almost there." He swayed in his seat. "Couple minutes." Ice ended the video call.

Liam said, "Let's go out and meet them."

Pronto was over by the tunnel to the outside, standing alert and still.

Roxie whistled, just a short note, but Pronto knew what it meant.

Instead of turning and coming to her, the K-9 started to back up. Roxie met her halfway and clipped the leash back on. "What is it?" She ran her hand over the dog's head, scratching her ear and one side of her neck. "What do you smell?"

She had already been on alert. Could be anything from a rock falling to a squirrel to an army about to attack them.

"I'll go first." Liam slid the weapon on his hip out of the holster and held it by his side.

Dirt drifted down from the ceiling. Up ahead, daylight spilled into the tunnel. One of the lanterns on the ceiling swung side to side.

The faster they got away from the nuke, the better. But it was also their job to secure it and make sure the thing wound up in the right hands.

Liam stopped at the end of the tunnel, keeping to the shade on the left while he looked out.

A bullet slammed into the side wall of the tunnel on the right.

A warning shot.

Liam flinched. "Someone is out there."

From what it sounded like, there was more than one someone. Pronto had been right to alert her, not letting her guard down for a second.

They would have to fight to get out of this.

It was far from over.

TEN

L iam held out his hand so neither Roxie nor the dog ventured forward. He'd protected them this far, and he would continue to do so. Whether Roxie agreed with everything he said or not. He figured from her reaction, there was some kind of issue with his heartfelt confession.

Lord willing, they would have plenty of years ahead of them to talk it over.

But that wouldn't happen if they got shot here and now.

"They must've stuck around to make sure it went off?" Why would anyone do that? It didn't even make sense. "Martyrs?"

"Gotta live for somethin' or you die for nothin'. Isn't that how it goes?"

"Something like that." Liam inched closer to the opening and tried to see out as much as possible. "I just can't remember if it was General Patton or Rambo. Or both."

All that effort to disarm a nuke, and they were going to get shot as soon as they tried to get out? No.

Adam and his friends were on their way, but that didn't mean help would be here in time.

Liam needed to know how many people were outside.

He peered out, gun first. Just a hot second, and he ducked back in.

More than one person fired. Two. Maybe three.

"Think we can take 'em?"

Liam wanted to chuckle at how adorable she was. But then, if he made a comment about Soldier Barbie —like the other Marines had on occasion—he would end up like them. On his back with a bloody nose.

He'd been forced to write her up for it a time or two himself, as her sergeant.

Now she was on his side, he didn't want that to change. So he kept his thoughts about her to himself. "Left and right?"

"With Pronto as a distraction?" The note of fear in her voice was strong enough he could hear it.

"We cover her, she covers us. That's how it goes, right?"

The dog put herself at risk every time they went out, just like Liam and Roxie did. The difference was that she didn't get a choice. If she didn't want to do the work, she wouldn't be a K-9. No handler had time for a dog that refused an order.

"Pronto." Roxie unclipped the leash and gave the dog a command in German or Czech. He didn't know what the language was.

Liam heard Pronto start to breathe heavily, like she was raring to go. "I'm left."

"Copy that. On three."

He let her count. The second she said three, he

went first. Hopefully whatever fire there was, he would draw it first.

Pronto raced past him, faster than Liam could ever hope to run.

Gunshots rang out.

He spotted a shooter to the left and squeezed off a shot. One buzzed past his ear in a way he didn't like at all.

Someone yelped, and he heard them hit the ground. Pronto growled like she did when they played tug. Roxie took a knee and fired off two shots to the right. Liam scanned around them while she raced to Pronto. "Out!"

The man screamed.

Roxie called out, "Pronto, heel. Don't go for that gun. Hands where I can see them!"

Liam wanted to look at them at work, watch the show like a spectator at a demonstration. Instead, he kept his attention on the area around them and spotted the gunman to the right of the opening. Roxie had winged him, but he got back up clutching his arm. Gun in hand.

Liam saw the intention in the way the man lifted his weapon and aimed. He stacked his hands and squeezed off two shots.

The man fell down.

Roxie said, "You good?"

"Clear." Liam jogged to her.

The gunman Pronto had downed stared up at them from the ground. "You should be dead."

Liam said, "You should've been trying to get as far from here as possible, considering you just armed a nuclear warhead underground."

It wouldn't have made a difference though, considering they would never have been able to get far enough fast enough to survive the blast. Or the fallout.

His brain had fought to assimilate that information. In the end, they had nothing to lose by trying to disarm the bomb and everything to gain when that attempt succeeded.

Thank You, Lord. They'd survived.

The whole thing was unbelievable. Not just evidenced by the man on the ground who barked a laugh. "A nuke? You're crazy. That was just a bomb."

Liam and Roxie stared down at the man. Pronto barked.

The man flinched. He kicked his legs out making ruts in the dirt with his boots. "Don't let that dog near me."

Roxie kicked the gun a little farther away. "Then don't threaten her. She's entitled to defend her own life, just like any cop."

Liam said, "Who told you it was just any old bomb?"

"Well, it weren't a *nuke*, that's for sure." He didn't lift his hands from the dirt. There wasn't much hair on the top of his head, but it hung down over his forehead. He wore dirty jeans and a denim shirt with a T-shirt under it.

Liam stared at him and said nothing. Roxie did the same. Were there any more out in the trees, waiting to kill them? Someone had to have been outside the cave the entire time. That must've been why the men inside knew they were coming—because someone outside alerted them.

"That's ridiculous." The man practically sneered at them.

"When our friends show up, they can take you down there and show you the inside of the bomb right before they return the materials to the government." Roxie glanced at him. "Or maybe we should do to him what he was planning on doing to us."

Liam caught her tone and knew she had no intention of killing this guy without a better reason than that. Still, the guy didn't need to know. Maybe it was better for him to believe they were miffed—and that one of them had a screw loose.

Liam shrugged. "We can say he went for his gun."

"Hey!" The man sputtered. "You can't just shoot me."

Roxie set a hand on her hip. "You were gonna blow us up."

"With a nuclear bomb, bro." Liam needed him to comprehend that he had been deceived—if that was what'd happened. He doubted this guy was that good of an actor. "You were lied to."

The man on the ground absorbed that.

"Whoever paid you to be here or ordered you to leave that bomb down in the cave, I'm guessing they didn't tell you this was a suicide mission."

There was a lot of information they needed from this man. From who he was, and how he ended up here, to what he knew of Darwish and the rest of the plan. Were there others in different areas planting bombs in a similar way? How many people would die if they couldn't disarm all the devices the way they had just now?

His heart still raced with all that adrenaline pumping through his system.

"You're lying."

Liam shrugged. "I could be, but I'm not. I have no reason not to tell you the truth right now."

"Who are you guys?" The man looked between them.

Roxie said, "Homeland Security Taskforce."

A car engine revved, and gravel sprayed. Liam looked long enough to see a gray Suburban pull into the clearing. The second he turned back, dirt hit him in the face.

Roxie yelled something. Had she been hit as well?

Liam blocked it all out. He tackled the man, who had gained his feet while Liam rocked back from the handful of dirt in his face.

The man hit the ground again, this time with Liam on top of him. Liam's gun went flying...he didn't know where. Pain radiated under his cast.

He grabbed the guy with one hand. The guy grabbed him. Liam fell back to a muscle memory that drew from not just time in the Marine Corps but high school wrestling. Even with all his injuries.

Liam shifted, and the guy grabbed his leg, probably a reflex to protect his vulnerable parts. Liam dropped his hip on that side, leaning into it. He threw his legs back at the same time, lifting his knees so he ended up with the toes of his boots finding purchase in the dirt. He used the hard surface of his cast to get a lock on the man's head and grabbed just above the guy's elbow with the other, effectively stopping him from doing anything else.

"Hey, that was pretty slick, Slick." Might've been Ice, Liam couldn't tell.

"All right, hotshot." Definitely Adam. "Let him go. We've got this."

The guy struggled under him, but Liam kept a strong hold even though his entire body hurt. His injuries couldn't seem to decide which was worse, as if they needed to compete for the most painful.

He wouldn't be in trouble if he didn't move, but with any move, there had to be consideration as to the wellbeing of one's opponent. That had been mostly when Liam competed. This was real life, and the stakes here were far higher. But still, he had a moral code.

Someone had to, or it would be the Wild West out here, and law enforcement might as well be private mercenaries.

Liam bit out one word. "Rox?"

"Got you covered." The pride and warmth in her voice was the only reason he let go. Liam saw four guns on the man under him and got out of the way of their aim. He touched Roxie's cheeks and saw dirt in the corners of her eyes. "Okay?"

"Yours is probably worse."

They needed to get cleaned up. Liam glanced at Adam. "Water?"

Adam tipped his head to the SUV. "Cooler in the trunk."

Liam snagged Roxie's hand, and they walked together to the SUV, Pronto beside them. Now that he didn't have a fight to focus on, each time he blinked, it felt like sand in his eyes.

She opened the back of the SUV, and he glanced over. Adam had the man on his feet, two handfuls of his shirt holding the guy upright more than his own ability to stand.

Others of his team had disappeared, presumably into the cave to take care of the device.

This entire situation was unreal. "I need to call Talia back, update her." He palmed his phone but couldn't read the screen.

"Tip your head back, babe." Roxie twisted the cap off a water bottle. Pronto had hopped up into the back and lay down, her paws stacked on the edge, looking around. Keeping watch over them.

Liam looked up. Roxie poured the entire thing across his eyes, going back and forth until it was gone. "Thanks." Liam resisted the urge to touch his face and wipe off the water. "That's much better."

She held out another bottle. "Hands."

He rubbed them under the stream, then helped her wash up. Which, of course, brought them close to each other. Alive. Breathing. Together.

He nudged her nose with his.

Roxie smiled. "We should probably postpone celebrations for later."

Later didn't mean after the case was done, so there was hope it wouldn't be *days*. But he doubted they could relax when a bomb could go off any moment.

Just thinking about it had him rolling his shoulders, stomping his feet to try and get rid of the slow burn of frustration in every nerve ending.

"Let's go see where Adam is at."

Liam said, "You go ahead. I'll call Talia and catch up."

He sat on the tailgate and let out a long breath first, giving himself a second. He rubbed Pronto's head. "Good girl."

The dog let out a contented sigh, yet in her relaxed demeanor, he could tell she would be ready to go again at a moment's notice.

And that was precisely what might happen.

Liam put the phone to his ear. "All clear, Talia. Adam's team is here, the bomb is defused, and we might have new leads."

"Good, Adam can have the scene," she said. "You're being redeployed."

ELEVEN

R oxie shook her head and held her hand out. "Keys."

Liam barely argued, handing over the keys to the rental. He looked tired. They'd been in a fight, and he'd been in that explosion recently. Who knew how hard he was pushing himself to ignore whatever might not be quite healed? Not to mention all the injuries he had that'd barely begun to heal.

She whistled, and Pronto hopped out of the back of her brother's SUV. The dog raced over and jumped right into their rental.

She got the K-9 all secured and shut the back. Her boots crunched the gravel, and she spotted Ice and Ash coming out of the tunnel with a heavy crate between them. They were securing the weapon and would hopefully return it to the government so it didn't fall into the wrong hands.

Roxie gave Ice a two-finger salute. She probably should have run over and kissed his cheek, but all these macho guys and her husband with that protective streak would flip out. Best to keep her gratitude to herself.

He lifted his chin.

She slid into the front seat of the car. Liam had his head back, his eyes closed. "Okay?" Boy, it felt good to be the one asking him that, rather than the other way around. Then again, the fact he'd been injured at all wasn't all right.

Neither of them liked to feel as if they were the helpless one of the two of them.

She programmed the GPS with the address Talia had sent—a hospital where someone had been admitted with radiation burns. After ten minutes of quiet and feeling antsy, squeezing the wheel, she called Simon.

He picked up on the third ring. "Olson."

"It's Roxie."

"Oh, hey." His voice softened fast, moving from surprise to the warmth that should characterize their friendship.

"When were you going to tell me that my brother is alive?" She gripped the wheel and tried to stay calm in her driving, while the residue of all that adrenaline coursed through her. She tapped her left foot on the ground, keeping a beat no one else could hear. "We talked about him, and you knew."

She'd kept a photo of her brother on her desk when she worked at Vanguard. Simon and his twin brother Peter had both asked her about Adam. They hadn't given her any indication they were lying. But that was what made it hurt all the more.

"He didn't submit his DNA. He doesn't use the last name Helton." Simon spoke carefully, stating the information but not in a way that made it seem like he felt the need to defend himself. "Does he look anything like your brother used to?"

"So you've met him in person?"

Simon said, "I've seen him on a video call. He stays off the grid for the most part."

"How many teams no one knows about does Vanguard have?"

She heard him chuckle. "Maybe best to not ask that question."

Roxie said, "Because I don't work for Vanguard anymore, so you can't admit the truth?"

"You signed the same non-disclosure agreement I did."

Roxie didn't even know what to say to that.

"Are we good?"

"Depends," Roxie said. "Did you look for what happened to Liam when I thought he was dead."

"I asked Adam to get you to call me."

"There's a difference between 'hey call me' and 'hey, I think your husband is actually alive.'"

"That's what I told Adam to say!" Simon huffed. "Did he not? Because he and I are going to have words about his access to certain tech that I designed, programmed, and constantly update when they break stuff if he didn't tell you Liam was *alive*."

Roxie let out a breath. "He thought he was protecting me." After what Adam had said to her about Liam, she wasn't all that shocked that he'd been the one to withhold that bit of information. "But he'll get the picture if he hasn't since."

The question was, did she need him to warm up to Liam? It would be nice to have his support at least. Not lying by omission and leaving her in her grief so she could what...move on? Surely she'd have realized Liam was alive sooner or later.

It hadn't been a solid plan.

And couldn't be the one that concerned her right now, since Darwish and his brother were plotting to destroy half the country.

She said, "Since he owes me...you can pass on every update he's got for Vanguard to me so that the taskforce can be in the loop."

"You think he's working the case and not telling you what he's got going on?"

Roxie said, "I think I keep leaving him with leads. So what's he coming up with? There has to be a way to get ahead of this. They're using locals, lying to people. There's a trail. We should be able to backtrack and find someone who knows where they are. Or knows how to get ahold of them."

Simon mumbled something about GPS.

"Do they have those phones that can't be tracked or traced?"

"You mean, the ones I designed?" Now he sounded downright grouchy and like he didn't want anyone to overhear him. The line shifted and he said, "I'm fine. It's Roxie." Simon paused. "Because she called me, and no. I—"

"Roxie?"

She smiled a little. "Hey, Pete."

"Are you okay? Is Liam okay?"

Liam said, "We're fine."

She glanced over, but he hadn't opened his eyes. "Whatever you need to say, do it fast. We're almost at the hospital."

"You're not fine! Who is hurt?"

She chuckled. "We're interviewing a guy admitted with radiation poisoning."

"Oh."

Simon said, "See? She's fine."

"I'll call you guys after the interview. Give you the highlights. But the minute Adam calls with information from the guy who nearly just killed everyone within hundreds of square miles, even if he didn't know that's what he'd be doing, I want to know what he said."

Silence was her only answer.

"This isn't a debate."

Silence.

"Guys, I want full disclosure. This isn't something we can mess around with." As far as she was concerned, how Adam felt about her husband was irrelevant until the case was closed. After that, she'd decide if she cared or if he would come around.

It wasn't like she needed him to walk her down the aisle.

We already did that.

And yet, Liam wanted to do it again for all their friends and family to see. She'd had no family when he asked her. So what had been the point? Now she had her husband back. It seemed right to celebrate life. Theirs. Everyone's. Why not have a huge party? That actually sounded like a great idea.

But renewing their vows?

Right now, it would only feel like going through the motions for everyone else's sake. Another reminder she had no friends that weren't his and no family to give her away to him.

"Fine."

Roxie didn't know which one of them had said that.

"You call us, or we'll call you," Peter said.

Simon said, "If the patient you're interviewing

has a phone, don't try to access it. Just call me. I'll walk you through something."

"Something like what?"

He paused.

Liam said, "Sie."

"This is only because it's you guys. I'm not telling two feds. I'm telling my friends."

Roxie wasn't sure it worked like that, but still she said, "Tell us."

"I wrote the program for their phone system. The one that can't be tracked or traced."

Her stomach flipped. She'd already known that, so what was he saying? "You mean, if I get you access, we have a shot at answers?" Had he really put a backdoor in the system?

"Yes."

The line went dead.

Roxie spoke aloud the question on the tip of her tongue. "Did he design it before he got his life straight, or was it one of his teenage forays into a life of crime?"

Liam shifted in the seat, rolling his shoulders as best he could in the tight space. "I hope Vanguard didn't ask him to create that as a side project. Remember how Talia said she's been trying to crack it on the side, working the problem?"

"I think we need to get the two of them on the same page." Roxie's life intersected where Vanguard met the federal government. She wasn't confused about what side she was on, but still the tug of loyalty was there. Vanguard had been a safe place to land, where she'd found support and friendship that was a whole lot like family.

She'd done the same thing with the Marine Corps.

Found family.

Now, he sat in the seat beside her.

Roxie pulled into the hospital parking lot. "We should let Pronto do some business on the grass over there, then crack the windows and let her sleep some more."

Liam shifted in the seat again, this time angling toward her. "She'll be all right."

"She isn't any less banged up than the rest of us." Roxie smiled. Liam reached over and tucked hair behind her ear, tracing the edge of her hairline. She said, "I'm sure I look great."

They'd poured water on their faces, and the dirt she'd rolled in during that fight was still all over her—and the seat of the rental car.

"Beautiful as ever."

She said, "I wasn't angling for a compliment."

"I know. Maybe I am."

Roxie laughed. "You know you're handsome enough it's seriously distracting, and then I wonder why I ever agreed to work with you." She rolled her eyes. "The team is probably amazed we get *any* work done."

Liam chuckled. He gave her a quick kiss and tugged a beanie over his hair and the four stitches on the side of his head. He grabbed the door handle. "Come on, let's go."

Ten minutes later, they walked into the hospital and introduced themselves. The receptionist directed them to the fourth floor nurse station and the wing of the hospital that had been designated for patients with contagious diseases. The place was nearly empty, except for the first room on the right.

Roxie stared through the window that ran the length of the room between the wall and the door. A nurse in protective clothing stepped out, and the door hissed. It sealed, keeping any contagion inside.

The nurse pulled down her mask, and they flashed their badges. "Right, they said you'd be coming."

"How is he?" Roxie met her halfway, wondering how they could get anything without going through a lengthy procedure and also putting themselves at risk.

"If you mean, is he able to answer your questions, that's not going to happen." The nurse sighed. "He just took a turn and lapsed back into unconsciousness. There's no way to wake him without causing him severe discomfort. So don't ask."

Even if it could be worth forcing his body to wake just so they could find out if the chance he knew anything might pay off, it was still morally gray. Regardless of how the information could help a lot of people.

Roxie nodded. "It was a long shot that he would be able to provide us with information, but we had to try."

"Because he exposed himself to nuclear material?" Her curious expression flitted between them.

Liam said, "Did the patient have any belongings on him? We have a warrant." He showed the nurse his phone screen, white with tiny lines of text.

"Everything he came in with is in a contamination bag. I'd recommend not exposing yourselves by opening it."

Roxie said, "Was there a phone?"

The nurse nodded. "That's among his things. I'll get the bag."

"Thank you."

She wandered off, and Roxie turned to the window. The patient had severe burns and was almost completely covered with bandages and the blankets. Machines flanked the bed, and multiple tubes had been connected to his body.

"Hopefully, we can get something from the phone. Or this is going to happen to a lot of people."

Roxie reached out and entwined her fingers with his. "Let's make sure that it doesn't."

TWELVE

L iam set coffee in front of Roxie. They'd both showered and changed clothes, coming back to the conference room to find Talia typing away on her laptop keyboard faster than Liam had ever seen anyone type.

"Thanks." Roxie leaned forward toward the screen of her brand new laptop—courtesy of Talia—which Simon had them connect to the patient's phone. The mouse moved of its own accord, so Liam figured he'd connected remotely.

"Is Vanguard allowed access to our federal computer system?" Liam sat, glancing between Talia and Roxie.

Niall was on his way back, and Dakota and Josh were coming down from their room. Pronto lay on the floor with her back to the wall, paws in the air, twitching—which Liam took to mean she'd appreciated him throwing the ball for her to chase.

Talia said, "Dakota's boss called Clare at Vanguard. Given the situation, it's been agreed we should all share information."

Roxie glanced at him, and he caught the look in her eyes.

"Adam didn't call you back yet?"

"Whatever he's working on, he's keeping it close to the vest."

Liam had been afraid of that. "Sounds more like we're sharing, but Vanguard isn't really reciprocating."

The laptop screen flickered, and Simon's face popped up in a window on one side. Through the speakers, he said, "Adam is following up on the lead he got from the guy at the nuke site. He said he isn't going to waste time calling when he has nothing. Yet."

Roxie sipped her coffee.

"I'm lucky he told me even that much. The guy doesn't respond to texts, and he barely picks up the phone." Simon shook his head. "He has some old school ideas, and I call Ice if I need to connect with the Renegades. Adam might be hard to reach, but he gets the job done."

Liam rested his arm on the back of Roxie's chair. "And what job is that exactly?"

"Whatever needs to be done." Simon sniffed. "Half of them should be in the Accountant's Office program."

Liam had heard of that but thought it was only rumors. Burned spies or special forces soldiers that had prices on their heads. The Accountant's Office was supposed to give them a clean ID and a way to live their lives under the radar where their enemies couldn't find them. A kind of private witness protection for people whose faces were too recognizable.

"The other half probably can't ever assimilate

back into civilized society. They know what they're good at, and they know they don't fit. They're aggressive and lethal. But they're also good. And sometimes, that's exactly what we need."

Simon paused.

Then he continued, "Roxie, you should know... your brother put in paperwork requesting you be added to his team."

"When he was withholding the fact Liam was alive." She reached over and touched his knee, leaving her hand there.

He shifted his fingers to the skin above her jacket collar.

Simon winced. "I think he wanted you to work with him."

"I'd have fit." Roxie cleared her throat. "Because without Liam, I would've been lethal. Feral."

Talia made a noise in her throat. "Good for you, girl."

Liam frowned. "You think that's a good thing, T?"

She shrugged, still typing at break-neck speed as she said, "I'm all for being a strong, independent woman. Y'all know I can hold my own."

Liam figured that was an understatement. There was no one better at computer stuff—except maybe Simon. She had more style than most people could fathom and rocked at being a mom.

"But." Talia lifted one manicured finger to make her point. "If anything happened to Mason or my kids, I would become homicidal in a heartbeat. Any of them. Or any of you, for that matter. Watch how fast I'd burn it *all* down if someone hurts you."

Roxie sniffed. "Talia, that was the sweetest thing." She swiped away an imaginary tear.

Liam grinned.

"Test me, you think I'm not deadly serious." Talia took a breath. "Hey, kid?"

On their laptop screen, Simon said, "Yes, ma'am?"

She chuckled. "This thing is scary genius. You and I need to talk."

Simon didn't look exactly proud. Liam figured if it was him who had designed a program that allowed bad guys to continue to commit crimes and get away with them, he might not be super proud of himself either.

Simon said, "I'd like that. I figure it's better to be your friend than your enemy."

"True dat." Talia chuckled to herself. "D's here."

The door opened, and Dakota and Josh came in. The dogs sniffed each other, and Josh instructed his K-9 into a "down." Neema let out a sigh, her head on her paws.

"Ambulance was a bust." Dakota huffed. "What's the latest?"

Liam turned the laptop so Dakota could see Simon and the work he was doing on the phone.

"Get me up to speed, Vanguard." Dakota pulled her chair up across the conference room table. Niall came in and poured himself some coffee. He sat over by Talia.

Simon said, "The phone is part of the clandestine communication network that allows them to operate separate from any known cell signal. They don't use towers. It's all internet based. It piggybacks off Wi-Fi signals, and satellites, taking whatever is within reach and accessing the connection without anyone ever knowing or being able to tell it's happening."

Dakota blinked. "That's crazy." She glanced at Talia. "That's crazy, right?"

Talia said, "Crazy like trying to destroy half the country with nukes? Or just pure genius?"

Liam figured it was more like the person who came up with the idea for a nuclear bomb in the first place, and the argument of whether it ever *should* have been built. His mom had drilled into them the old adage, "just because you can, doesn't mean you should." With three teenage boys, that had been sage advice. Just because they had the freedom to do something didn't mean it was wise.

Simon's upbringing had been quite different, so Liam wasn't going to fault him for not always doing the right thing. What mattered is what he did *next*.

Dakota said, "I'll let someone smarter than me decide that. Simon, can you access the network from this phone?"

"They work on a tier system. This one is lower level. Others have access to everything, so getting our hands on one of those would be the golden ticket to everything Darwish is telling the people he's giving orders to. All their communication."

Liam lowered his coffee cup from his mouth. "That would be great."

"If we knew who had them." Simon sounded a little sardonic. "But I can get a decent amount from this one, including the fact that there are three bombs. And I'm guessing he doesn't know we took custody of one."

"Two still in play?" Liam leaned closer to Roxie, not ashamed of the need to feel the same solidarity she reached to him in order to find. "We have a better idea of where, but what about when?"

That was the most important thing for them to learn. When would Darwish be detonating them, and where did he plan for them to go off?

There were more locations to look through from the dead professor's notes, but it could take time they didn't have to search everywhere.

"Seems like the patient was a student at Cal Tech. He had someone close to him, and while he built the bombs—or assisted that part—the friend, brother, whoever it is, was employed to deliver one."

Liam's eyes widened. "Simon, does he know that the patient is out of play?"

"He's been texting, asking what's going on. Why your patient isn't answering."

Liam looked at Dakota. "We need to set up a sting."

She nodded. "Good idea. Send a reply, say he was tied up and busy. Ask to meet. Say he wants to join up with the one out with the bomb and see the end of this."

Roxie said, "Our guy by the caves didn't know that the bomb was a nuke. This guy has to, since his friend was the one building them."

Liam said, "There's a lot of need-to-know going on. We could say he needs to tell the guy something important, but it can only happen in person."

"I like this idea." Josh nodded.

Niall said, "Me, too. We can set it up and make sure he doesn't get away. That'll be two bombs out of play."

Roxie turned to Niall. "You think he'll have it with him?"

"He'll tell us where he left it. And how much time we have," Niall said.

"It's scary to think we could be too late. A lot of people are in danger." Roxie shivered.

Liam squeezed her neck. Roxie's experiences gave her a deep empathy for those who were powerless to fight against their fate. But he'd also seen her get back up when anyone would've been knocked down for the count.

She would make an amazing mother someday.

If the team—and Vanguard—could stop Darwish, there would be more than enough reasons to celebrate. Whatever form that took, he wanted to invite her into his family in a way she would know they had claimed her as one of their own.

Should Adam want to be part of that, in some limited way, Liam could extend a hand. The guy might not take it, and they would likely always butt heads when it came to certain things, but Liam was prepared to set aside his pride for the sake of her blood. Her brother.

Dakota said, "Simon?"

"You tell me what to say, I'll make it look like it came from him." Simon paused. "I'm sending transcripts of their conversations to your email, so you can match the wording pattern. He's less likely to get suspicious if it sounds like his friend."

"I'll draft something up, but we need to move quickly." Dakota glanced over to the side. "Talia, anything we need to know?"

"I've been running through options for where Darwish might go with Carim to hunker down while all the chaos and destruction is happening."

Roxie said, "You think he'll run?"

Talia shrugged. "I wouldn't stick around. I'd get as far away as possible. So I've been thinking through escape routes, places far enough he can see the explosions but not be caught in them. Planes are out. Boats are too volatile. He'd need somewhere remote with a lot of miles but line of sight."

Liam said, "Alaska?"

"Or even the east side of Russia," Talia said. "Beringia National Park. Or St. Lawrence Island between Alaska and the Russian coastline. It's accessible by boat. They could get there in a few hours from Seattle."

Roxie looked up from her phone screen, and he spotted her maps app open. "The Aleutian Islands are closer."

Liam connected some dots. "But Darwish had Russian friends, sympathizers to his cause. He could be planning on connecting with them and getting himself safe harbor on their soil. He probably would just want to get across the Bering Sea as fast as possible."

They'd extensively studied Darwish before their team had gone in to take him down. Liam knew all about the man's friends then. But who knew him now? That was the question.

He liked the idea of baiting a trap for one of the men transporting a nuke. That seemed more in his skillset than alerting the Navy to a threat. "Roxie and I will work on the texts with Simon."

"We can alert the Navy to someone looking like they're trying to escape." Dakota glanced to the side. "Niall?"

He stood. "On it." Niall strode from the room.

Dakota lifted her phone and started typing. "Anyone else got any other good ideas?"

"Other than scouring mountainsides for bombs, which we probably don't have time to do, I can't think of much else." Josh shook his head.

Dakota said, "Then let's get to work on what we have."

THIRTEEN

Roxie paused on the park path and bent to re-tie her sneaker. She didn't give Pronto her normal command to sit, which confused the dog and meant she acted more like a pet and less like a trained K-9. "Good girl," Roxie whispered.

Entirely different to the meet in the park with Carim—and not just because this was a completely different park in another city—Roxie wasn't the one waiting.

Liam sat on a bench, one knee bouncing. She thought it was cute, whether or not he intended to look impatient.

Roxie straightened and continued on her circuit through the park, with Pronto by her side. The team had scattered around the grassy area. Over the tips of the skyline of buildings, the sun set on Eugene, Oregon. She passed two older teens, getting a little hot and heavy on their blanket. Roxie kept walking, content enough to do her job—giving those two kids the freedom to make mistakes and grow, to learn things and experience life on their terms.

She didn't do the job she did only for the sake of good people.

Like the Bible said, about the rain falling on the just and the unjust alike. If they succeeded, they'd be saving the lives of civilians whether they were innocent or not. People had the right to choose their own lives. Her jurisdiction was the authority her badge gave her, which wasn't to judge someone else on Roxie's own convictions.

The truth was the truth, whether people believed it or not.

"Girl, you got some deep thoughts going on in that head of yours." Talia's chuckle sounded warm in Roxie's ear.

She smiled, catching sight of Dakota and Josh walking Neema together. Seeing them hand in hand, no weapons in sight, no badges on display, made them almost look harmless.

Almost.

No one would mistake them for people who couldn't take care of themselves.

Thank You. It might seem like a strange thing to be grateful for to some, but for Roxie being part of this team and working alongside these people let her know she could fit in. She could belong to something good outside of her faith.

The body of Christ was a little ethereal, and she could appreciate with sincere gratitude that this team of predominantly believers in Jesus had chosen to include her. It meant they'd seen worth in her.

Which hadn't happened to her much in her life.

Roxie said, "Love you guys."

Dakota's attention whipped around in Roxie's direction, though that was the only indication she'd heard what Roxie said. The team leader leaned close to Josh, linking her arm in his and leaning her head on his shoulder in a way that said she was completely comfortable. "Statements like that tend to precede cavalier actions that get the job done but put your life at risk. I get mad, you get written up, and everyone agrees they would've done the same, but they also wanted to be in the loop so they could help."

Roxie nearly smiled. She worked to keep her face impassive and spoke low into her radio, "I'm not planning on running off and saving the day alone, even if I thought I could. I just appreciate you guys taking a chance on me."

Roxie tossed a tissue from her pocket into the trash and took a second to look over at Liam on his bench. He lifted his right hand and laid it over his heart, then abruptly stood.

She frowned, caught herself, and kept walking.

Coming toward him was a dark-haired man, olive colored skin. Pretty cliché for a man employed by Darwish, who had so far hired local petty criminals to do his work on the ground and keep his hands clean.

"Got him," Talia said. "Your instincts were right, Lee. He's on a watch list, and there's a warrant out for his arrest."

The man wandered toward Liam, looking around. For his friend who'd sent him the texts summoning here—a man currently in critical condition.

Liam checked his phone, like any guy at a park might.

The man closed in.

The rest of the team started walking toward the two of them, including Niall who she spotted dressed as a vagrant, and closed the net so the guy couldn't slip through.

Talia said, "Hakim Farouth. Libyan and a supporter of terror groups du jour. He's not particular, he'll fight for whoever. Suspected of war crimes. Wanted by Europe and the FBI."

"Shame we don't have an agent on our roster. It could've been handy," Dakota said. "By the numbers, everyone."

Roxie said, "Copy that."

Niall echoed her statement.

Liam approached the man coming toward him but looking for someone else. "Hakim? Our mutual friend sent me to pick you up and take you to him."

The guy froze, and Roxie could tell he was about to make a run for it at any moment.

"He can't get away. You understand he's busy."

Hakim looked like that proverbial deer in the headlights. "He would've told me if he was sending someone else."

Yep, definitely gonna run.

Liam drew his weapon. "Federal agent. Stay where you are. Keep your hands where I can see them."

Roxie picked up her pace to a run, and Pronto trotted along beside her. She slid her weapon free of its holster.

The others did the same, surrounding Hakim. He looked around at them and seemed to realize there was no use in running.

Josh approached him. "Don't move." He got Hakim in cuffs, and everyone moved their badges to their belts so no one around them wondered what was happening.

Roxie turned and scanned the area in case a sniper had already set up. Unlike last time, she didn't want anyone to get hit.

When Liam touched the small of her back, she set off walking, keeping her attention on the buildings and trees with line of sight. Car windows. Storefronts. People who could draw a weapon at any time.

They escorted Hakim to the van. Josh held the door while Dakota walked Hakim inside where they had a chair set up across from Talia's workstation.

As soon as the door closed, Liam turned and kissed her forehead.

She figured she knew what that meant, given his response to her confession. The out loud realization that she was where she was supposed to be. He wanted to give her a family, but it didn't always happen like that. She had the sense of being in the right place with this taskforce.

It was enough.

Who didn't want to be content with where God had placed them?

Roxie figured that was the whole goal. And if they could get this plot stopped, that would be a huge bonus. They'd know they saved potentially millions of lives. *You can do that. You can lead us where we need to go to stop this.* She prayed they'd get information they could move on from Hakim. He seemed like the kind of guy who might be closer to the inner circle, knowing the bomb maker and all.

In the end, all she had was the truth of who God was, and a whole lot of questions.

You alone are God. He was the one who could help them defeat this evil, intent on destroying so much. *Your will be done.*

Liam wound his arm around her. "Praying?"

"I don't think I've quit being grateful or asking for help since I spotted you in that other park." She smiled up at him, their faces close.

"I know what you mean." He touched his lips to hers.

The back door opened, and Josh stepped out. "The bomb is already armed, but the timer isn't a timer. It's a receiver. Darwish controls the detonation remotely via the network, so there's no way to jam any signal since we don't know how they're connected."

And it was ready for him to set them off at any time? Roxie winced. "That's not good."

"Understatement of the year." Niall took off the threadbare beanie he'd been wearing. "Where are they?"

"He only knows where his is located," Josh said.

Roxie wanted something to do, a mission to undertake, but there was a better resource for this. "We should tell Adam's team. Have their guy, Ice, who knows about nukes, disarm it."

Josh nodded. "Talia is calling them."

Roxie blew out a breath. "What about the other one? There are supposed to be three, right?"

Josh's jaw tightened. "He doesn't know. We need to find who does. What he *might* be able to give us is information on Darwish. His phone is a tier up from his friend. He's closer to Darwish's inner circle than the bomb maker."

Now that was interesting.

"He claims Darwish said something about a plane to take him to his promised land." He frowned at Liam. "You good?"

Her husband leaned against her more than he normally would—as if he needed her to hold him up. "Just need to sit."

Roxie looped her hand through the leash and turned to grab his elbows. Liam's cheeks flushed. Was it just a result of pushing himself too hard in his state, or had he been hit with a substance that was attacking him?

She said, "Did Hakim do something to you? Or did someone else give you something?"

"Juss...light. Headed." Liam started to go down.

Josh and Niall jumped in to catch him, tugging him into the van. Pronto danced around them, reacting to the fear they were putting off. They laid him on the floor in the van, and Roxie spotted Dakota by Hakim. Talia on a rolling stool at the desk. The middle aisle cleared as they made space for him, though there was little room.

Josh said, "He passed out."

"I'll call an ambulance." Niall set a hand on her shoulder.

"Is it his head?" Roxie bit her lip. Was he having some kind of aneurism? "He shouldn't be pushing himself so soon after being blown up, but he seemed okay, and he didn't say anything."

Dakota swayed on her chair.

Hakim started to smile.

She swayed too far and tumbled onto the floor, unconscious.

Josh said, "Everyone out of the van." He shoved her and Niall away. "Neema, *out*. Talia, you, too."

Talia slumped onto her keyboard, and one arm flopped down by her hip.

Roxie backed up, taking control of both dogs.

"You feel okay?"

She nodded in answer to Niall's question. "What is going on?"

Josh climbed out of the van and touched Neema's head. "*Sitz.*"

Roxie said, "Pronto, sit."

The two dogs sat close, probably needing the proximity while they waited to see what was wrong.

Neither of these two men had answered her. "Did Hakim come here intending on poisoning us?"

That meant he had to have known they weren't his friend in the hospital.

Another thump in the van rocked the vehicle.

Josh pushed the door wide, and Roxie peered in. Hakim thrashed on the floor, foam coming from his mouth. A gleam of satisfaction and humor in his eyes.

As if he'd won.

No.

"We need to get them out in case he gave them the same thing." She gasped. Liam had been more vulnerable to the close proximity, probably because he was recovering. Or some reason which meant he had been more susceptible to whatever toxin he'd been exposed to.

An ambulance turned the corner, lights and sirens blaring. Niall waved to it. "Over here!"

Roxie turned to the van door.

Josh got in front of her. "Stay out here. We don't need more casualties. We need hazmat. And an infectious disease protocol." He put his phone to his ear. "You have the dogs, I've got them." He thumbed over his shoulder, and she saw in his eyes that he understood exactly how she felt.

This was bad.

Lord, help us.

FOURTEEN

Liam sucked in a breath and immediately tried to sit up. He didn't get far. His body refused to move, choosing to be sluggish while his mind eclipsed in sheer panic. The explosion. *Roxie*.

All he could think about was how he'd woken up, and she wasn't there. Even when he hadn't remembered who he was, thanks to the bump on his head, he'd known there was someone who should be there with him.

Having his mom there had helped, but Roxie had been missing.

He'd found her.

He'd...

A blonde woman was curled up in a chair by the bed, a blanket over her all the way up to her chin. Tucked around her shoulders. Hair fell over her face, and she breathed in long slow inhales and exhales.

Liam shifted in the bed so he could lay there and just absorb the fact she was here. He was here. Things were okay—not like the last time when the panic had been real and not just the residue of a memory.

His elbow snagged, and the tug shot pain up to his bicep. An IV. The bag hung beside the pillow, nearly empty of whatever they had given him. A drug to... His mind managed to recall the van, the man he'd met in the park.

He'd gotten woozy, and when things slowed down, he hadn't been able to stand. Or stay awake.

What about the rest of them?

If Roxie had been dosed with the same thing, however he'd been exposed to whatever it was, she didn't seem to need the same treatment. Because she hadn't been in that explosion, and he had? Neither of them were fans of being vulnerable, but he preferred her to be the healthy, safe one. Meanwhile, he wanted to be the stronger one so he could protect her. Didn't exactly make sense, but there it was. They could be equals, and he could still want to take care of her at the same time.

On the far wall, the TV flickered. Tuned to the news channel with the volume muted. The clock on the wall indicated it was after eleven, which meant he could've been unconscious for a couple hours, or more than a day. With the sunlight behind the blinds, it was definitely nearing lunchtime.

Liam hit the button to raise the head of his bed.

Roxie stirred, blinking. Pushing her hair back and shifting the blanket to her lap as she woke up. "Hey."

"Sorry. Didn't mean to wake you." She needed rest as much as they all did. Though, he did want an update. They had a serious situation on their hands, and lying here wasn't going to solve the problem. "But I could use an update."

Roxie nodded, shifting her angle on the seat. She

looked at the screen of her phone. "Okay, nothing new in the last half hour."

"How long have I been out?" She must've just dozed hard for a nap if she'd only been asleep thirty minutes or so.

"A couple of hours. They said exposure to the neurotoxin wasn't life threatening, though it did knock out you, Dakota, and Talia. They were probably trying to take us all out." She frowned. "They said your condition meant you succumbed faster. Dakota and Talia were in the van with him. I don't know if they're awake yet."

"And Hakim?"

"He's dead," she said. "And the patient with radiation poisoning didn't make it either. He passed away earlier."

Darwish and his actions had cost a number of lives already, and he didn't seem to intend to slow down. Not with nuclear bombs hidden wherever. They couldn't even be certain they knew how many there were.

Bottom line was, if something was going to go down, he would face it with Roxie by his side. And their K-9— "Where's Pronto?"

Her expression softened into a smile. "Snoring in the car. I've been going out periodically and letting her walk around."

Liam nodded. "How long do I have to stay here?"

She frowned. "Long enough that the IV bag is empty and the doctor clears you. So don't even think about leaving before then."

She might want him to believe it, but this couldn't be a reprieve. She probably wanted him back up to being fighting-fit. He doubted that would happen before this was over, but maybe the drug they were giving him was a miracle thing.

He could rest without being impatient.

To a point, anyway.

He said, "Have you heard from Adam?"

"Just Simon." She sighed. "He got into the phone to a point. They shut it down before he could use it to piggyback all the way to Darwish, but he's working on getting back in. He asked for any help Talia can give him when she wakes up."

She glanced aside for a second. "Niall wasn't affected, so he called Talia's husband, and then he went to check out one of the locations the professor came up with. He's got teams of federal agents looking at all of them. After this attack, no one on the team is prepared to allow this to get out of control. We want every fed available working on this."

Liam nodded. "We have confirmation that Darwish has nukes in his possession and the intent to use them."

"Exactly. Talia's husband is leaning hard on the powers that be to push all resources to this. They understand what we're up against now, so a lot of people are being sent to help us. There are agents up and down the coast looking for Darwish, Carim, any nuclear devices, and at all airports, ports, and train stations."

"In the aftermath, he'd have to be out of range of the discussion."

A smile lit in her eyes. "We had that conversation already. The feds have that on their radar, mostly ATF and the Marshals. They're the ones looking for Darwish and Carim. The FBI is taking point on nukes. You know the FBI, they're all about the glory."

Liam returned her smile. Then he asked again, "Have you heard from Adam?"

Her expression shifted like she'd been caught. "Fine. He hasn't called me back. And it had *better* be because he's close to something. Or has a plan that means there's no time to risk jeopardizing it with a phone call. Not just because he doesn't like you and he's mad."

"You don't have to worry about my family, by the way. They already love you." He motioned with his fingers for her to come near to him.

She pushed aside the blanket and sat on the edge of the bed, winding her fingers in his. "I'd love to say he'll come around, but maybe he won't."

Liam wasn't sure he actually cared. He didn't need Adam's approval or his permission. He and Roxie were already married. If that sounded a little alpha male, he didn't plan on apologizing for that either. It was his job to keep her safe. To make her life good.

Adam's discontent with their relationship didn't help, but Liam wouldn't let it bother him.

Her brother seemed intent on believing Liam was just like the other men who had been in her life. Maybe it boiled down to the fact that, as her brother, he hadn't been able to be there to protect her. Roxie thought that was because he'd been dead. But being alive and unable to tell her might actually be worse torture.

Liam had enough empathy in him to feel for the guy, but if they were going to be friends, it would take some work.

Roxie leaned down and kissed his cheek. "I'm glad you woke up."

"I'm glad you were here when I did." The fear he'd felt wasn't something he wanted to go through again.

"I should go tell the nurse you're awake." She started to shift off the edge of the bed.

Liam's attention caught on the TV. "What the...is that Darwish?"

"It is. On the news?" Roxie grabbed the remote from the side cabinet and turned up the volume so they could hear what he was saying. Across the bottom of the screen, the words *BREAKING NEWS* scrolled over and over again.

"...time for America to cease holding the world in a chokehold. We will not live by values you yourselves do not live by. You talk of freedom but know nothing of honor." Behind General Darwish was a brick wall, just generic red bricks. Nothing else was visible.

No way to tell where he was.

He continued, a darkness that looked a lot like death in his eyes. "This 'great' country pillages the world, spouting words of hope when under cover of darkness, they send soldiers to take the lives of those who work only for the future of their people. The world needs America to leave us alone."

Roxie reached for Liam's hand again. The feed looked like a social media broadcast being relayed on the news, but the top right-hand corner of the screen indicated it was *LIVE*.

They were the soldiers that America had sent.

Liam and Roxie and those they'd been on a team with. Marines on a mission to take out a dangerous man who had *never* worked for the future of his people.

He had only destroyed it.

"The world needs America to stop sending soldiers and spies to assassinate heads of state and freedom fighters for their own benefit. America is officially on notice. We are deadly serious in our resolve. To that end, we have hidden a number of nuclear devices up and down the west coast. Should you fail to comply with our demand, we will detonate those devices. Millions will perish. Millions more will suffer. The fallout will be catastrophic."

Carim's plan.

Darwish had his brother and intended to carry it out.

But the last thing Liam had expected was an announcement of his intentions. Darwish must believe there was no way they could stop him. So, what was the purpose of this announcement other than to send people into a panic?

Roxie's hand squeezed his. "What does he want?"

Liam held on tight to her hand while Darwish continued, "America will release all their political prisoners. Every single one. Within the next twenty-four hours. Or you will never bother the world again. Your resources will divert to the domestic chaos I will bring upon you for generations to come."

Darwish paused.

"Failure to comply will result in devastation. The bombs are already armed."

Roxie half-whispered, "Maybe he doesn't know we have one."

Darwish said, "Your twenty-four hours begins *now*."

The screen went dark, and a speechless news anchor's image came back up. "Ladies—" She cleared her throat. "Ladies and gentlemen, you heard it live on TKOG Channel twelve. A madman will destroy the west coast if the government refuses to release all political prisoners."

She blinked. Swallowed. "You heard it here first." She paused again, then said, "Local governments are requesting all civilians to remain at home. If you decide to leave the area, please do so with consideration for others. We are all in this together."

Roxie hit the mute button. "Political prisoners?"

He was more worried about rioting, airports in chaos with grounded planes. Freeways blocked with streams of traffic. Everyone trying to get as far away from this as possible. "It serves his purpose. But he already got Carim." Liam's mind spun. "Does he really care about all of them?"

"This whole thing is about making a point. A statement."

He nodded. "And he's going to murder millions in order to get his message across."

"Niall will come up with the nukes, right? I mean, we disarmed that one. We can get to the rest in time."

Liam wanted to believe that as much as she wanted to. "If even one goes off..."

She looked at him, something like terror in her eyes. "I know."

He sat up, leaning forward. "We have to get out there and stop it."

FIFTEEN

Roxie strode into the hospital room next to Liam's. "Talia isn't awake yet." She pulled up short.

Dakota held her phone to her ear. She waved them in. "Yes, sir. Absolutely, sir." A few seconds later, she hung up.

"Sorry." Roxie should've paid more attention to her entry rather than barging in. That announcement had her...she couldn't even describe how she felt right now.

Liam shut the door.

Dakota said, "It's all good." She sat in bed, hooked up to an IV as Liam had been. She wasn't finished with hers. But she might as well be at her desk, with the laptop in front of her and her phone in one hand. "Talia isn't awake yet?"

Roxie shook her head. "Mason is on his way."

"Josh took Neema to help Niall. Neither of us likes doing nothing so at least he can help."

Liam stuck his hands in his pockets. "Recovering from the effects of a deadly substance you were exposed to isn't nothing. It's *recovering*."

"Agreed." Dakota pointed to the chair. "So sit."

Liam crossed the room with a huff of a laugh and settled into it. He didn't need to be out running, chasing down bad guys anytime soon. But she also couldn't see him being content to sit here resting.

Roxie said, "What's the latest?"

Dakota winced, shoving some of her long black hair behind one ear. "The governors of the nearest five states called an emergency meeting. Most of them are getting their leadership as far away as they can, or to secure locations. But they want to detonate an EMP or two, or more, at strategic locations I'm supposed to help coordinate with them."

Roxie said, "EMPs?" Wasn't that some kind of device that didn't cause destruction necessarily, but it would shut down all electronics. Basically sending everyone in the blast radius back to the stone age.

Dakota nodded. "They want to kill Darwish's ability to detonate the nukes. We've briefed them that with them being armed, and him having a phone on that system, we have no way to shut them down without finding them...or a total blackout so Darwish can't send the signal that will cause them to blow. And they want to kill the electronics on the warheads at the same time."

Roxie could see why they'd chosen that route.

"Okay." Liam tipped his head to the side. "Kinda desperate, considering how many lives could be lost. Pacemakers. Surgery suites. They're going to kill *everything*?"

"It would be a last-ditch effort," Dakota said. "And no one likes it. The federal government wants to veto the whole idea. The president doesn't like the plan. He wants other options presented to him, but the governors are digging their heels in saying this is the only way—so long as all other options have been exhausted."

"There isn't much time to come up with another idea for them to consider." Roxie leaned against the wall, thinking it through. "Any movement on identifying what political prisoners he's talking about, making moves so it looks like we're complying with the demands?"

She of all people knew you couldn't negotiate with a bully.

Dakota shook her head. "No one is interested in that, except as a last resort. There's probably someone working on it, but I have no idea."

Roxie had gone toe-to-toe with her abuser—and his brother—and there had been no convincing them. People like Darwish had a plan, and they expected people to simply comply. A man like Darwish might not necessarily care about political prisoners. It could be an impossible problem to set America spinning trying to placate him when he had no intention of backing down. Which meant the governors' plan was a smart one.

It could be a last-ditch effort that paid off and saved a lot of lives.

A man like Darwish...

He was a bully, just like her ex. They'd run into each other accidentally, and he'd kicked Pronto, giving the dog cracked ribs. If she ran into him again, things would end differently.

She wanted to.

Did he even care about her and Liam? She figured they had to be on his radar at least, or why would Hakim bother to target them like he had with whatever substance it had been? The doctor gave her the name and explained it was a poison, but not a nerve agent. Something aerosolized so that they only had to stand in proximity. Physical touch—like putting cuffs on him—had made it worse. But not all of them had fallen victim to it.

Something else to talk with Darwish about if she got the chance.

Watching that news broadcast of his statement, she'd half expected him to mention her and Liam. They were his enemy! They were the ones the government had sent to kill him years ago.

Why hadn't he called them out?

It could have seriously hampered federal law enforcement in their attempts to find him and take him down.

Roxie's phone rang.

The two of them broke off their conversation that she'd tuned out.

"It's Adam's number." Roxie put in on speaker. "O'Connell."

For a long second, he said nothing. "That's the name you're going with?"

"You didn't call to discuss me taking my husband's name, did you?" She held the phone but didn't look at Liam, not wanting to know if she was right about what look would be on his face. They needed to stop Darwish, not get caught up with other things —like her being mad the guy didn't care more about her and Liam.

It was probably better that he didn't as they could likely move more freely this way.

He probably thought Hakim had slowed them down.

"No, I did not." Adam sighed. "I need your help. Simon needs your help."

He knew how to get her to listen. "What do you need us to do?"

"Not him. Though I figure he'll come with you. This mission needs a woman with uh..." Adam cleared his throat.

"Okay, I get it. What's the job?" She made the mistake of glancing at Liam. The look in his eyes said he wanted to grab the phone and throw it out the window—after he told Adam, "Heck no." But he didn't get up.

"It's a longshot, but two of my teammates are escorting the first warhead to NORAD in Colorado, and Ash looks bad in a skimpy dress."

Before she could ask what that meant, he continued, "Without Talia to help, Simon's got Peter, but there's still not much they can do without a phone that is unlocked at that higher level of the criminal network Simon needs access to. All we have so far is lower tier phones. But we know of someone who has a top tier phone."

"So, the phone gets you access?" She could steal a phone, couldn't she? She'd never pickpocketed anyone before, but if the scenario was set up correctly, she could get close enough to distract a man while she or someone else nabbed his phone. "Once you have the phone, Simon can use it to find Darwish?"

"Exactly. If we get this phone, we can breach the system. Simon thinks he can disable Darwish's phone entirely. Or crash the whole network. Either way, he won't be sending any messages that set off bombs."

"That sounds like a good tradeoff for wearing a

dress." She glanced at Dakota, who nodded. Then Liam. He didn't seem as convinced as their boss, but she figured he wouldn't want to be anywhere but with her when this went down.

Liam called out across the room, "Who is it?"

Adam said, "Figured you'd ask. The movie producer, Carlton Shepps."

Roxie winced. "Great."

"Nope. No way. I'll do it." Liam swung up out of the chair and strode over. He didn't grab the phone, but she could see it took everything in him to keep his hands by his sides. "She's not going anywhere near Shepps."

"We need that phone." Roxie spoke gently, not wanting to sound like she was arguing. She just had an extremely valid point. "We need it so Simon can end this. It might be the only way, and I might be the only one who can get us it."

"If he even carries it with him all the time." The fire in Liam's eyes was about protecting her, and she loved that about him. "Adam, this guy is suspected of murder. He's being looked at for the disappearance of a number of young women and girls."

"I don't suspect him," Adam said. "I already know he's guilty."

Liam didn't like that answer.

Roxie said, "It could be the only way to end this."

"It's Roxie's choice," Dakota said.

Liam spun around.

Dakota lifted a hand before he could say anything, and she continued, "But the two of you are partners in work and life, so it has to be both of your choice. I could order you to assist the Renegades, but I won't. Not even in this situation."

Liam gave her a nod, then glanced at Roxie.

She said, "Simon needs this to end what's happening." She knew what it would mean to her friend to bring this whole plot to a conclusion. To deny Darwish what he wanted. A man like that? He was everything Simon despised.

"How are you going to get close to him?" Liam shook his head.

Adam said, "Simon got into his company emails. He ordered a woman from a company that provides that 'service,' so he has a friend for the inflight hours. She's supposed to meet him at his plane at a private airstrip outside Napa in a couple of hours. We don't have much time to get you there."

Liam winced. "She's supposed to get on his plane? If he takes off, he'll figure out pretty quick she's not what he ordered."

That was true enough, she figured. It wasn't like she could get too deep into a ruse where she was a hired companion. Two seconds after he touched her, she would have him in a headlock on his stomach on the fancy airplane carpet. "You know I can hold my own."

"That is never in question. I know what you can do. I've seen it." Liam touched her neck the way he did that she liked—where she could feel the warmth of his palm on her skin. The comfort that felt like support and the need to be close to her at the same time.

"I've got an outfit for you and a car for you to drive to the airstrip," Adam said. "We don't have much time."

Roxie asked her brother, "Do we have anything else we can do? Any other plans or options? Leads to follow?"

Maybe if there was another option, Dakota could suggest that instead. Or Liam could help figure out an idea that might be more fruitful.

"This is our best shot." Adam's tone invited no argument.

That didn't necessarily answer her question, but she was satisfied enough with his answer. He'd never been a liar even if he had willingly withheld the truth. She wouldn't be holding a grudge when she had Liam back.

Adam said, "Bring your dog with you."

And he hung up.

Roxie figured that was that. She wanted a full brief from her brother on the particulars of the mission, but given how much information he'd given her before she'd been standing in that park with Carim, she figured it was unlikely he'd share much. Liam wouldn't let him get away with it.

Adam probably figured she'd balk if he let her know the risks.

He'd learn pretty quick she could be tough when she had to be. Like facing down a man like Carlton Shepps. It wasn't going to be pleasant, but she would get that phone. After all, she would go in knowing her husband and her brother—and his men—had her backs. In no way was she going to be alone.

After all, millions of lives were on the line.

"Be safe. Both of you." Dakota lifted her chin.

Roxie nodded.

Liam said, "Let's go before I change my mind."

SIXTEEN

Liam ran from the fence, where Adam had dropped him, to the back door of the hangar. Carlton Shepps' airplane was inside, the jet set to depart in just minutes. With Roxie on board.

Nope.

He patted his pockets again and pulled his gun just in case, keeping it in a loose hold by his side. In the door, through a hall with a bathroom and back offices, all decorated in seventies style military décor and which smelled faintly of cigarette smoke.

On the far end, he looked through the round window and then snuck out into the hangar. Three guys, one in a pilot uniform and the other two in jumpsuits and reflective vests watched the car pull in. Adam drove a low-slung muscle car with blacked out windows. He'd changed into gray slacks, a mustard color silk shirt and gold chain around his neck, and shiny black shoes.

Even though he looked the part, Adam didn't get out of the car.

The passenger door opened, and the first visible skin on Liam's wife was her thigh and knee.

She angled out of the door in heeled boots, a tiny skirt, and a crop top. More makeup than she would wear in a year and hair she'd "teased," whatever that meant. He didn't look closely, but she'd done something to her eyes that made her look hopped up on something. So Shepps would think she might be compliant—if he was into that kind of thing.

Liam set aside all of it and got to work. The alternative was wading through this hangar, punching people left and right, and jeopardizing their chance of getting the phone.

If the plane got going with Roxie on board, and he couldn't stop it, she would suffer in ways he wasn't prepared to live with.

Thankfully, the three guys were staring at her, not paying attention to the square metal storage container that had been packed with all their food and beverages that needed to be loaded on board.

Liam climbed onto it and up into the storage hold.

He palmed the first tube of liquid cement and squeezed it into the hinge of the open hatch so that when they went to close it, the mechanism would malfunction. They couldn't fly with a compartment in the back that couldn't be shut.

He did the same on a computer panel he found with a USB port, squeezing more liquid cement in, hoping it would mess with their electronics.

Liam followed the faint voices, moving through a door to where a woman in uniform—presumably the flight attendant—bent to offer someone a drink on a tray. He wasn't sure if her pinched face displayed a displeasure of Shepps, or the fact he'd requested another woman and not her. The way she offered him the drink suggested she wanted to be chosen.

The attendant straightened, glancing at Roxie who had stepped onto the plane.

He watched through the window. The flight attendant headed for him, irritation on her face, and he had to duck out of the way.

But he couldn't escape.

She was coming toward him.

Liam turned to the side and ducked out of sight. As soon as the door swung shut behind her, he approached. One arm around her neck, he pinched her in a hold he kept gentle just in case. He only needed her to pass out. He didn't need to hurt her.

She tensed and started to bat at his hold on her. Nails scratched at his forearm, but this was a hold he'd done many times. She wouldn't be able to resist for long.

Her grip slipped off his forearm.

Her movements sluggish.

Liam lowered her to the floor, unconscious, and made sure the door wouldn't hit her.

He heard a muffled, "Hey!" from the main compartment and headed for it. A man strode down the center aisle toward him, pulling a gun.

Liam waited a second until he got closer and then shoved the door out, smacking the man with it, and barreled through the door.

Beyond the suited man who'd spotted him, Roxie stood in front of Shepps.

The movie producer shifted out of his seat to greet her, which forced Roxie to take a couple of steps back. Shepps grabbed her wrist.

A hold like that would squeeze small, delicate bones.

Liam's suited attacker swung his gun. This close there was no point trying to squeeze a weapon between them. Liam raised his arm up fast and swept the hand out of the way, then kneed the guy in the stomach.

The man doubled over.

Liam grasped the man's shoulder and brought his knee up again, this time in the man's face.

Bone crunched. He collapsed to the floor, and Liam stepped over him, headed for Shepps. Roxie needed to get that phone. If he could distract the guy...

Liam lifted his gun and took a couple more steps toward the man, refusing to look at Roxie. "I don't like you. I have no reason to let you live."

He didn't need to see the pain or discomfort that might be on her face, and neither did he need to draw attention to her.

Shepps had a round face and extra meat under his chin. He filled out the suit, but the tailor was good. "What do you want?"

He spoke with all the authority of a man who got whatever he wanted because he had the cash to pay for it.

"Your pilot owes me money," Liam said. "So step aside, and I'll go talk to him before y'all leave. Get what's mine. Then I'll be gone."

"And I should then forget you were ever here?" A gleam of something entered Shepps' eyes. "I don't think so."

Three men stepped onto the plane, all wearing suits like the guy he'd already dealt with. Not one looked friendly or prepared to give Liam a pass. Let alone go easy on him.

Shepps said, "Get this plane in the air. We can drop this one out the door when we reach altitude." He seemed to find that exceedingly amusing.

Roxie let out a tiny whimper that seemed to surprise her.

"The lady and I will be busy, but maybe she'd like to watch us dispose of you."

Liam shrugged. "Maybe she would."

None of them seemed bothered by the fact he had a gun. Why was—

Heavy weight slammed into his back, and Liam's gun hand hit the armrest on a chair. The cast wedged under him when he fell. He got a face full of carpet and heard Roxie make a noise. Pain sparked in his head, eclipsing his thoughts. Muscle memory kicked in, and he got his arm back, wrapping the guy in a hold that held him to Liam's back while he rolled.

There wasn't enough room in the aisle to execute the full move, but they rolled, and he scrambled around. His left hand was free, so he punched with that. The guy's jaw felt like the concrete that liquid cement dried into.

Someone chuckled.

Liam grabbed the guy's head and slammed it against the seat, knocking out the second man. Three to go.

He launched up and met the first one running.

They collided in a tangle of grappling and grunts. He heard Roxie, then someone yelped. *Good for you, babe.* She was holding her own—or he hoped she was.

Liam focused on the fight in time to see the

punch coming when it was too late to bob his head out of the way. The fist hammered into his temple.

It washed over his vision. Pain exploded like a firework in his face, and he stumbled back two paces before he caught himself on a chair so he didn't go down.

He braced for the man to follow up and finish the fight—with Liam unconscious or dead.

Instead, the guy turned his head to look at the door.

Liam wanted to shoot the guy but instead just shoved him into the two others. All of them slammed against the wall by the open door.

But they didn't come at him again.

Shepps had Roxie on his lap, and she didn't look happy about it. Blood dripped from his nose, but he wasn't letting her go. "One of you deal with *this*. The rest of you go outside and find out what's going on."

That was when Liam heard it.

Multiple vehicles. Men yelling. A few gunshots that pinged off the roof of the hangar.

Two of his suited opponents stumbled out. One was shot right away, stumbling and falling down the stairs. The other ran back in.

Liam looked around quickly and found his gun.

He swiped it off the floor right as a man ran at him, and Liam squeezed off a shot. The guy collapsed against him, but Liam turned and pushed the guy to a chair. He landed half sprawled on the floor between rows.

Dead.

Shepps shoved Roxie off his lap, and Liam saw her tuck something in the back of her skirt. "One of you protect me!" He looked at Liam. "Get the door shut. I'll fly you to safety."

One of his suited men, presumably bodyguards, drew his gun and headed for the door. He angled his gun out first and fired a few times. Rounds came back at him, pinging off the hull of the plane. Embedding in the side.

"Stop shooting!" Shepps yelled. "Get us out of here." He moved to the front and hammered on the closed cockpit door. "We're leaving now."

Someone poked their head out, a uniformed pilot in a white shirt with a gray mustache. He said, "Sir, they are blocking our exit and threatening to destroy the plane if we don't let them on board."

Liam motioned to Roxie. She ran to him, and he grabbed her hand. Liam swung her in front of him and spotted the phone in the back waistband of her skirt. "Go. Go."

She raced through the swinging door toward the flight attendant.

A shot pinged off the wall beside him. Liam ducked his head. "Go."

The exterior hatch was still open. Down in the storage hold, she sat and levered herself off the opening.

"If you need cover, go for that crate."

She nodded but said nothing. Though, he did see her reach back and check the phone was secure. Liam held his gun, jumped down, and immediately turned three-sixty. A jumpsuit guy, presumably an aircraft marshaller since he had two of those reflective wands in one leg pocket, spun toward them.

Someone fired a shot, and it hit the guy square in the chest.

He went down, falling on a hose that was connected to the underside of the plane. The hinge yanked apart, and gasoline started to spray out, glugging like a water hose all over the floor around the man. The tang of fuel permeated the air.

"There are at least ten of them," Roxie said. "They want the plane?"

"They can have it, right?"

She nodded. "We have what we came for."

Liam looked around. No one seemed to have noticed them, or if they did, they failed to care. "We need to make a run for that back door. Or the side."

Roxie sucked in a breath. "Where is Adam?"

The car was gone even though he'd said he would stay long enough to get paid as per their fake agreement with Shepps' people. It figured he'd split before the trouble started.

"Go. I'll cover you."

Roxie squeezed his side as she turned and raced for the door. Liam stuck close to her, not willing to be separated. They barreled through the door to the back hall. She raced along to the exit door, only wobbling slightly in her heeled boots.

Liam could admit to being a little distracted by her outfit. He cleared his throat. "Maybe those men were looking to leave the area, and this is how they've chosen to do it."

She shoved outside into the bright sunlight. Adam's car pulled up along the fence and stopped.

Her brother rolled the window down. "Let's go!"

An engine revved behind Liam.

His foot caught on the uneven grass, and he tumbled to the ground just as more bullets started flying.

SEVENTEEN

Roxie got out of Adam's muscle car for the second time in a matter of a couple of hours, this time from the back. Liam slid over and got out behind her, and she heard Adam get out his side. Her brother had angled the rearview mirror away while she'd changed in the backseat. Liam had handed her jeans and a top that covered her midriff. She pulled the white leather jacket over it, being surrounded by it giving her a sense of comfort.

Liam looked at her, the question prominent enough in his eyes.

She nodded since she didn't have any immediate problems.

Adam opened his laptop on the flat part of the trunk lid and set a phone on either side. One was the phone she'd pickpocketed from Shepps. The other was his phone. He tucked earbuds into both ears and peeled off the silk shirt. "Get me a T-shirt, Rox?"

She ducked her head back in the car and grabbed the one he'd removed earlier. It didn't smell great, but it wasn't ridiculous like his pimp outfit.

She handed it over, and he tugged it on. Roxie spotted a number of scars that were bullet holes—or they had been. One of them hadn't been sewn up by a professional. He'd been in a couple of scrapes, maybe knife fights. And she spotted a strip that looked a whole lot like a burn scar on his lower back.

If Adam knew she was staring at him, he didn't acknowledge it.

"Hey, Sie." He typed on the laptop keyboard. "Yeah, she did great."

Liam scanned the vicinity around them. She caught his muttering, "No thanks to you."

Roxie shook her head. "Before I went in, he gave me some good advice."

Liam turned to her.

She wasn't ever going to convince him that her brother was a good guy, was she? Roxie slid her arms around his waist, not losing her view of their surroundings. "He made sure I was prepped and knew what to do if things went sideways."

"Did that scum bag touch you or say anything you didn't like?"

She assumed he was now referring to Shepps, and the involuntary shiver just thinking about that man wasn't something she could hold back. "I'm okay. We got the phone."

He might never like it, but if there was ever a time that qualified as extenuating circumstances, the threat of nuclear explosions was it.

Fear was like a sour feeling in her stomach, constant. She wouldn't be able to get rid of it until Darwish had been stopped.

"People are running scared."

She looked around at what he was seeing. Folks

lined up to get gas, the queue out the gas station and around the corner, backed up onto the street. Practically blocking the intersection. Others were in line for the freeway entrance behind them, where a steady stream of cars drove slowly, trying to get as far east as fast as they could. Escaping the threat.

Still, a lot of people seemed not to even believe it was real.

Or they felt certain the situation would be resolved without them being at risk. Some folks might not have even heard, though she couldn't imagine being that cut off from what was happening in the world.

"That's what those guys at the airport were doing, right?" Roxie watched a couple of cars join the line for the gas station. "They wanted the plane?"

Liam nodded. "I'd rather have killed Shepps, but he didn't give me a reason to shoot him. You had the phone."

"You knew that?" She wasn't sure he'd seen her lift it from the movie producer's jacket.

"I saw it in your hand."

"Wow, I didn't even know."

Liam smiled. "If you think I pretended well, you should've seen yourself. It was pretty impressive stuff."

Roxie wasn't so sure of that. "I was panicking the whole time. I mean, what if he'd copped a feel? I'd have broken his wrist and kneed him somewhere special." She winced. Doing that would've ruined the whole mission. "Give me a weapon, boots, and fatigues, and I'm your girl. That outfit? Not a good career choice for me."

Liam's lips twitched. "Good look, though."

She rolled her eyes. Of course he would think that. Because he didn't know how uncomfortable she'd felt with so much on display. *Okay, he probably did.*

She was about to say something when his phone rang. Roxie's was in the car, but Liam had his phone in his pocket. He tugged it out. "Niall." He put it on speaker. "O'Connells."

"Hi, guys."

Roxie smiled. "Hi, Niall."

Her brother was deep in conversation, responding to whatever Simon was telling him to do on the phone. Head bent to it, typing. Trusting them to watch his back.

"Found another nuke."

Even Adam looked over, though he quickly got back to work.

Niall sounded breathless. "Eastern Oregon. In a cement plant, buried way deep down a shaft they had dug years ago. The whole place was shut down." He sounded like he was walking fast. "Anyway, we got down there, and it's been disabled. Same as what you guys said you did, disconnecting the detonator. There were a couple of agents with the FBI here who work ordinance disposal, and they called people they know at the Pentagon. It was a whole thing."

Roxie could hear how impressed he'd been by them in his tone. "That's great it's taken care of."

Liam said, "One more, right? As far as we know?"

"Right. The manifesto and intel Adam has given us agrees. Though, no one here knows about Vanguard's involvement. Except us." Niall paused. "On my way."

She got the feeling the last part hadn't been talking to them.

Niall said, "We're headed to the next location now. You guys good?"

"Yes."

Liam nudged her shoulder with his and gave her a warm look. "Adam and Simon are working on the phone."

"Copy that. Keep me posted." The line ended.

Roxie said, "Call Dakota?"

Liam nodded. They listened to the phone ring, and then it connected.

"Special Agent Pierce," she answered. "Though, after all this, I think I'm going to consider changing it to Weber at work. It seems to be working for you guys."

Roxie smiled. Dakota didn't use her married name at work since most people knew her maiden name. She'd married their team member Josh before she took over supervision of the taskforce, back when it was run by a woman who worked for the State Department that Roxie had heard about but never met.

"Okay," Dakota said. "Give me an update."

Liam ran down the plane, Shepps, and the phone in a few seconds. Then he said, "How is Talia?"

Roxie was so glad he'd asked, she let out a sigh. Their friend had still been unconscious from the effects of the drug when they left the hospital. Truthfully, she'd been worried there was something more serious wrong with Talia but hadn't wanted to say it aloud. As if giving voice to the fear would somehow make it manifest.

Words had power, but she didn't believe it worked like that.

Dakota said, "Talia is awake now. Mason is here, and the kids are headed to Grandma's in Virginia with a friend of theirs. Not ideal, being so far from your children and still in danger. No one is willing to leave their posts with so much at stake. Niall had Haley take their kids to his sister's and all of them are heading east. They're already in Eastern Wyoming because they left yesterday and drove all night."

Roxie said, "What about Liam's family?"

He shifted his stance.

"Right." Dakota paused. "That's up to the two of you. There might not be time for them to get out of Benson, and reports are coming in that airports are packed with people trying to fly east."

Liam said, "I've been keeping my mom posted. My brother and his family headed up to Alaska a couple of days ago. Mom should be joining them." He looked at his watch.

"I didn't know you'd talked to them."

Liam looked at her. "It was after the explosion at that black site. I explained the stakes. She called Conrad and Rory, and they made a plan to get Conrad's family safe. But the goal was to do that without inciting the panic we have now."

She saw in his expression how hard it had been not to call everyone he knew. Then again, he'd been focused on finding her.

She'd known what was going on but hadn't called anyone. She had only sat on the deck of that boat, staring at the water, drowning in her grief.

Maybe the issue with her and Destiny not connecting when her friend had suffered a serious trauma was also about Roxie. Not just about Destiny not calling to connect with her and get some support. Roxie hadn't reached out either.

She bit her lip.

Liam tugged her to his side, holding her close. She could see Adam looking at them out the corner of her eye but didn't want to worry about that right now.

"I'm going to pray they get somewhere safe." But the reality was that so many more lives were in danger. Good people who had families. Loved ones. The best kinds of friendships, the ones that defied blood and wound up defining you—like the way things had gone with Liam.

She'd never expected to have all she did now.

"When this is done, because I *have* to believe we'll finish this, we should go see them."

"In Alaska?"

She nodded, even though Alaska sounded cold. Maybe they were in a warmer part? "Yeah, can we do that?"

His eyes softened. "Okay." Liam touched his lips to hers softly.

Dakota spoke again, "Anything on the phone yet?"

"Sorry, we didn't forget about you." Even though she'd totally been distracted by her husband. It was that or face the reality of the situation they were in and the sheer number of lives that were at stake. Roxie glanced at Adam. "Anything?"

Adam nodded. "Simon is in."

She pulled away from Liam, and he came with her to stand by Adam. "Tell Special Agent Pierce."

Adam didn't look up from the computer screen. She didn't know what he was looking at. It was like nothing she'd ever done on a computer, all weird programming code—or something. She had no idea. He tipped his head toward the phone, and she realized he only wore an earbud on one side now. "Vanguard has access to the entire network. We're running down which phone most likely belongs to Darwish, but it's a needle in a stack of needles."

Roxie frowned. "Just shut the whole thing down. That way he can't set off the last nuke."

Dakota said, "I second that."

"If we do that," Adam said, "then we lose Darwish." But there was something in his expression that made her wonder if Vanguard could shut it down. "If we stop it then he knows it's over, and he goes underground, or he initiates some plan he has as backup that we aren't prepared for."

Liam shifted closer to Roxie. "So, what does Vanguard want to do?"

Adam lifted his head and looked at them. "Simon is writing a program that will create a communication delay. When Darwish sends the signal to detonate, Simon will be able to intercept it before anything explodes."

"And in the meantime?" Roxie knew that look in her brother's eye. He had a plan.

"We're gonna find him." Adam closed the laptop. "And then we're gonna kill him."

EIGHTEEN

"**Y**ou see it?"

Liam heard Adam's voice through his headset. It had taken far too long to get to this part of the country, and not just since they had diverted to the hospital to pick up Pronto. Roxie hadn't wanted to go into this without her K-9 for backup, and he couldn't blame her. Even Adam seemed to prefer it.

The pilot of the helicopter who had picked them up looked oddly familiar, but Liam didn't know Adam's team that well. The guy had given Roxie and Liam a polite nod. He couldn't argue with that, and this wasn't the time for personal issues.

There was a country on the line, as well as a whole lot of people.

Niall hadn't called to say they'd found the last device yet, but it could be anytime.

Right now, they had to find where Darwish and Carim were holed up on this mountain. Somewhere in the middle of Yellowstone National Park.

Roxie said, "I don't see anyone on my side."

Pronto sat in the back between the two of them,

tongue hanging out like being in a helicopter was so exciting. The dog wore a military-green bullet proof vest with FEDERAL K-9 on both sides. Liam had no idea where she got it but figured it was likely Dakota's doing.

Liam scanned the ground, his gaze finding an out of place item. "My side. Two o'clock. Looks like a vehicle. Maybe a van like the one at the mine."

"Satellite dish?" Adam asked. "Never mind. I see it. That's got to be him."

"Because of the dish?" Liam studied it, but the pilot kept their distance so Darwish and his brother didn't get a clue that they'd been discovered.

"They need line of sight to the satellite in orbit that can bounce off and come back down to hit the nuke, and with it using this communication network none of our signal jammers will work. It's a relay from the phone, up to space, and back down to the ground in Washington—or wherever the nuke is."

Liam would have preferred it to be as far from his family and his hometown of Benson as possible. *Lord, help us all.*

"I'm gonna go with trusting Simon on this one, because I have no clue about that stuff." Roxie chuckled, but there wasn't much strength to it. He didn't blame her. This whole thing was so far from funny, he wasn't sure if he would be able to let go and just laugh for a long time. Even if no one else died.

Adam said, "I understand the basics, but Simon is on another level entirely." He paused. "Yeah, over there looks good."

The chopper had a decal for the Bureau of Land Management, with a red tail and a red horizontal stripe. If Darwish knew anything about the western US, he would think they were only scouting for wildland fires out here in the middle of nowhere.

Not that they had found his hiding place.

The pilot set them down and they all climbed out. Liam left his headphones, and as soon as he closed the door, the helicopter took off again.

"Is he waiting to pick us up somewhere?" Liam asked Adam.

Roxie's brother said, "He's picking up the rest of my team and bringing them here in case we need backup. But it'll be a while. Let's go see what we can see."

Roxie stood, holding Pronto's leash. Ready to work, both of them were still with the kind of attention that said they were about to hit the ground running to go after this guy.

"It's amazing he hasn't set the device off yet." Liam chose to be grateful for every second they had to live, to be free—to work the problem. "Niall hasn't found the last one." He checked his phone. "Yet. But he thinks he's close."

"Then let's go roust out Darwish and his brother." Roxie lifted her chin.

Liam could've kissed her because he loved this side of her personality the way he loved all the others. She kept him on his toes. There was no one else he wanted to wake up next to. Whether that was at home, in a hotel on the road, or in a hospital.

Though, he knew which he preferred, and the scenario didn't involve him being lethargic from the aftereffects of a dangerous substance. Or recently blown up. Running on coffee and adrenaline.

Or all of the above.

"Let's go." Adam slung his backpack on his shoulders and shifted his rifle so it hung in front of him.

He looked like a hunter.

It just wasn't deer season.

Roxie walked beside Liam, and none of them moved slow. He tried to figure out how far it would be to the van he had spotted. How these guys had managed to drive it all the way up here without pre-mapping it out and making sure the vehicle could make it up all the inclines. Or modifying it for off-roading and finding a good dirt track to drive on.

In the end, he pushed all the thoughts out and just prayed.

God had been with them thus far. Why would He leave them now? Liam had survived what should have by all rights killed him several times over by now. Roxie was here. They were together. The team was all alive and either recovering or working the problem—or both, in Dakota's case.

Two nukes down.

One still to go, and it was looking promising.

"After all that time sitting in the helicopter, it feels good to stretch my legs." Pronto ran to the end of the leash and took care of some business. "Good girl."

Liam smiled at them. "Love you."

Roxie smiled back. "I know."

He managed to laugh at that.

"You guys are gonna make me barf, you know." Adam just kept walking, up ahead where Liam was surprised the guy could hear them.

Roxie said, "One day, you're going to fall in love, and you'll be all gooey about it, and we'll say we told you so."

Adam glanced back then, such a look of grief in

his eyes Liam's steps faltered. He heard Roxie suck in a breath. He said, "I don't have the luxury of 'one day.' All I worry about is today."

"Tomorrow isn't promised?" Was that what he meant?

Adam glanced through Liam and back around to face front. Evidently, that was all he intended to say about it.

Liam looked at Roxie, who made a face. She had no idea either apparently.

Lord, maybe he needs You. Maybe he needs to get the dream of love back. Hope for the future. That's the kind of thing You do, isn't it? Adam could use a whole bucketload of promise. If we survive this, then maybe You could work in him the way You have with the rest of us.

Minutes later, up a steep incline, Adam slowed to a stop, and they caught up to him. "I'm going around from the left. The two of you need to draw their attention. I'm going to get on the roof of the van and disable that dish so he loses connection. We might only have a few minutes, and if he sees us coming, he will detonate the nuke in a second."

Roxie said, "Simon can stop it, can't he?"

"Let's work like there's a chance he might not be able to."

Liam nodded. "We'll wait until you can get close enough and then cause a major distraction." In fact, he already had an idea. "Got any matches?"

Adam reached into the thigh pocket of his cargoes and handed over a package. "Three minutes." He turned and started to run in one move, sprinting with an impressive speed.

"He's like a whole different breed of person, right?" Roxie glanced over at Liam. "It's not just me?"

Liam smiled. "It's not just you. Come on." He led the way through the clearing to where they could see the van, not far off a dirt stretch that could be the road they traversed to get up here. The van sides were covered in a film of dirt, with bugs across the front grill. Curtains had been pulled around the front windshield and the two side windows.

He didn't spot any cameras, but that didn't mean moving into the open wouldn't get them spotted.

Pronto ducked her head and growled.

"Ooh, you smell payback, girl." Roxie kept her tone light, for the dog's sake. To Liam she said, "In training, there was a guy, a Marshal from New Mexico. I didn't care for the guy. Anyway, he stepped on her foot, and she limped for a while, but the vet said there was no damage. Just bruising. She growled at him like that the rest of the course."

"So what does it mean now?" That Marshal wasn't here.

"My guess?" Roxie said, "She can smell the man who kicked her."

Liam spotted Adam climb up onto the roof and slide along on his elbows. "Time to cause mayhem."

He grabbed a branch with a good amount of dry leaves and bundled it with a couple more in his arms. He skirted the edge of the clearing and shoved it under the van close to... He spotted it.

Liam tugged the cap for the dirty water disposal, and thankfully, nothing came out. *Thank You, actually*. The small mercy of dry pipes let him set the tiny fire fast, and he got it built up until smoke was billowing up into the hole. Given the first set of dry pipes, he chanced they'd been using nature to do certain business and unscrewed the cap for the other tank.

He didn't need to blow the place up, he just wanted to smoke the guy out.

Now the fire was going, smoke would come up through the drains in the sink...and the toilet. Liam lit more brush, shoved more leaves and twigs together, and kept lighting, creating a good size fire under the van.

Lord, please don't let this start a wildfire.

It would be a lot less of a threat than a nuclear blast, but no one wanted either.

Liam scrambled back out from under the van, coughing more than he wanted to. Though, the goal was to flush—hopefully—two men out of the van. He rolled over and scrambled up.

A door creaked open on the other side of the van, and the man who rushed out turned to aim a gun at the roof. He fired several shots at the man up there with a .45 Liam would've said was overkill.

Adam grunted.

Liam raised his weapon.

A gun went off from across the clearing, and the man shooting at Adam fell. Roxie had fired before he did. He heard her fire again, and might've spotted the muzzle flash, but couldn't see where she was. He raced to the front of the van and shouted, "Adam?"

"I'm good!" came the yelled-out reply.

Liam saw Darwish running into the woods, along with another man. How many others were with them here? Had it been just the three of them with the van?

He set off running after them and heard Roxie call out a command.

Pronto raced out in front of him. She hit Darwish full force and took him down. Carim angled left and raced between the trees.

Liam did the same, cutting off the path toward him so he didn't get between Roxie and her dog.

Up ahead, Carim stumbled and nearly went down. It gave Liam the chance he needed to catch up, a God given shot at victory.

He pushed to run as fast as he could, slammed into Carim, and sent him to the ground.

Carim's head bounced off a rock, and he was knocked out.

Liam landed off balance and rolled into it, coming up on one knee to the sound of his phone ringing. *Niall.*

"O'Connell."

His colleague gasped. "The bomb. We found it, but it just armed!"

NINETEEN

Roxie's back hit the ground. Pronto's growling surged in volume until all she could hear was that and the rush of air in her ears. After the dog took him down, Roxie had joined the fight. Now it seemed Pronto was eager to switch back again.

Above her, trees stood tall and still. It seemed odd, as if they should be moving. The tension of the situation shouldn't allow anything else.

Not when *everything* was on the line.

Thick fingers squeezed her neck. Darwish's face came into view above her, his teeth gritted—about the only thing she could see in the shadow from the bright sky behind him.

Roxie grasped and tugged at his hands.

She kicked with her legs, trying to get enough purchase on the ground to dislodge him and his hold on her.

Pronto barked, distressed that Roxie hadn't given her the command to attack. But it wasn't going to be her dog's life on the line. Roxie would much rather take the hit and be at risk than have to fear losing what she loved. Again.

She gasped.

No air passed through her constricted airway. Spots blinked black at the edges of her awareness, blurring what she could see and feel.

Lord. Help. She couldn't form words more than that. Couldn't grasp a thought. It seemed as though they passed by, out of reach. She needed Liam. She needed help. But she also reached deep inside and discovered a well of determination all her own.

The same drive that gave her the strength to crawl from a burning car and leave her life behind. Allow the pain of the past to fade.

The drive that would have had her working on Adam's team after Liam's "death." She'd probably have been almost feral. Still, she'd have attacked that life—the work he did—with a determination most people she knew wouldn't understand.

But God knew what the alternative was. The life she'd have lived. He had rescued her from herself and given Liam back to her.

"Roxie!" That was Liam, but he sounded far away.

Pronto grabbed a bite-full of Darwish's shoulder. The general cried out, tipping his head back. It jerked. She realized a second later she'd heard a gunshot.

Blood trickled from a hole in the center of his forehead.

He slumped to the side, and Pronto hopped over her to that side, growling and barking. *Platz.*

It was Liam who said, "Pronto, *out.*"

The dog backed up.

"Lay down, dog."

Pronto didn't want to.

Roxie blinked and saw nothing but sky again. She couldn't...

Liam's face swam in front of her. "Breathe, babe. You need to breathe." He leaned down and blew air into her mouth.

Her throat erupted in pain.

Roxie moaned, and he rolled her to her side so she could cough. It hurt. *So much.*

"That's it." He rubbed a hand up and down her back. "Breathe." There was a second of pause, and he yelled, "Adam!" More desperate and louder than she'd ever heard anything.

Roxie winced. Every breath was like knives in her throat. She pursed her lips and tried to ease the pain of her swollen throat, but nothing helped.

"Okay, we gotta go." Liam slid his hand under her and lifted her into his arms.

Her head landed against his shoulder.

Why couldn't she...

Roxie moved her hand. She flexed her feet. She tried to get as much air in her lungs as possible. Her brain needed oxygen. It was over, wasn't it? Darwish was dead. Carim, too, if Liam had come to save her.

"Pronto, come!"

The dog barked, but Roxie heard the jingle of tags go ahead of them. She turned to look but everything swam around her.

Whoa.

Nope. No passing out.

Liam strode faster than she could really process they were moving.

Adam rushed up. "What happened?"

"The bomb is armed." Liam lowered her to the ground, but in a sitting position so she could see her brother.

He shook his head. "I got the satellite off the van and disconnected." He frowned. "And I put out your fire."

"Well, *reconnect* the satellite because Darwish armed the bomb before I shot him. We only have a few minutes according to Niall." Liam held out a phone. "Get it reconnected, and I'll send the signal to turn it off."

Adam kicked up dirt he turned so fast. She could only watch as he raced across the clearing to the van and levered himself onto the hood, then onto the roof.

Roxie pulled in more air. She shifted her hand and held on to Liam.

"Hey." He shifted her on his lap and kissed the side of her hair. "It's gonna be okay."

She wondered if he needed to say that for his sake more than for hers. She knew God would be true, and *for* her, no matter what. Whether she had plenty or nothing. Whether she had a family or none. If she had Liam, or if something happened to him.

God would still be God.

He would still be good, regardless.

Peace she'd never felt before settled into her soul. It felt like it poured into her, restoring her strength and hope. Giving her life she hadn't ever known. A fullness she didn't understand until now.

And she couldn't make the words to tell anyone.

This is just for me, isn't it? Like a gift, the renewed sense that God was so very personal to *her* settled in her heart. Even when she had nothing, He cared for her.

Thank You.

Roxie watched Adam work on the satellite. Until finally, he turned and called out, "Try it now!"

Liam said, "Okay. Go for it, Simon."

Ah, he was on his phone. Darwish's phone.

The solution in his hands. *Thank You, Lord.* Roxie's family had brought the solution. God had guided them here and given them the ability to save so many lives.

"Done!"

Liam's loud voice made her flinch, and a noise emerged from her throat. She pushed off his lap and sat up, breathing hard. It still hurt far more than breathing ever should, but she tested talking with a few nonsense noises.

Adam called back, "We're good?"

Liam didn't answer right away. Then he said, "Simon says yes!"

Adam hauled the satellite dish off the roof and threw it over the side. It whipped through the air and landed on the ground with a thud, bending the dish.

Then he jumped off the roof of the van like it was a curb. He landed and bent his knees, then flopped over onto the dirt on his back and simply lay there. Staring up at the sky.

I've missed you.

Roxie wanted her brother in her life, as much as that was possible. She wanted him and Liam to be friends—brothers. Only God could work in them enough for them to be close, but even if she had to pray for a lifetime, she would beseech the Lord to do that work.

To give her the desires in her heart.

Pronto bounded over to her brother and lay down, her head on his chest. Adam put an arm around the dog and petted her while she wagged her tail.

"Okay, good plan." Liam paused. He lowered his hand, and she spotted his phone, which he thumbed to end the call and then immediately called Niall.

She lifted a hand, her index finger extended. Geez, this was taking a lot of energy. She tapped the speaker button.

Liam chuckled. "I've got it." He tugged her a little closer while it rang.

The second the call connected, Niall launched in with no greeting. "It reverted back to that square of lights going around and around, which I guess is it waiting for the detonation signal." He paused to let out a heavy breath. "We got the detonator out, so it's safe. And about seven thousand National Guard troops just showed up, so I'm pretty sure they're taking this thing into custody."

Liam said, "That's great news."

"What about the first one? They're asking who has it."

"That's the one Adam's guys were delivering to the military."

Roxie nodded along with what Liam said, because that was what she'd been told as well. It was what she knew to be true.

Niall said, "It hasn't shown up yet."

Adam lifted a hand and waved it, like waving off their concern.

Liam snorted. "We'll be sure and follow up. Make sure it lands in the right hands."

"Good," Niall said. "No one is willing to risk anything like this happening again." He paused. "Gotta go. You guys good?"

She nodded.

Liam said, "We're all good. But Roxie needs a hospital, so we're gonna go get checked out."

She made a face and felt him chuckle against her back.

"Roxie agrees with my assessment."

Niall said, "Later, guys," with a whole lot of affection in his tone.

"Yeah, bro." Liam hit End on the call.

Roxie tested moving. If she could prove she was moderately all right, maybe she didn't need to see a doctor. It was never fun to be poked and prodded. But at the same time, her throat was super swollen, and that was never a good thing to mess around with, even if it was only bruising.

"Adam's made a friend."

She smiled at her brother and Pronto, content to lay on the grass. "She's a fed." Her voice sounded like slow moving shale being poured out at a job site.

He squeezed her shoulder. "I'll see if there's water in the van." Liam jogged by her brother. "Call your chopper. We need a ride out of here. Roxie needs to see a doctor."

Adam glanced at her but didn't sit up. She waved. He lifted one hip and dug out his phone to make the call.

Liam came back, making a face. "It's nasty in there." He twisted the cap off a water bottle. "But this was in the fridge, and it's sealed." He handed it to her. "Take small sips."

Roxie nodded.

Liam stared down at her. For someone who'd just saved millions of lives, he should look happier. "I need to go and mark the two bodies so the police can pick them up."

Roxie had the bottle lifted, trickling water into her mouth. She made an "okay" sign with her other hand.

Liam leaned down and kissed her head. "Love you."

He jogged off.

Okay, so she'd scared him by getting hurt like this. Liam didn't like the part of the job where she risked her life any more than she liked when it was him. Roxie prayed a quiet prayer that he would find the same peace and rest in Jesus that she had.

This was a journey they would both be on, side-by-side.

Forever.

The sound of a helicopter reached her awareness, over to the southeast. Rescue was on the way. The threat was over.

Roxie lay back on the grass, watching birds fly in a V across the sky. *I see why Adam did this.* She put a hand on her chest and felt the rise and fall.

Still breathing.

Each one was a gift from God she had no intention of taking for granted.

Wind whipped around her. Roxie laid her arm over her eyes while the helicopter landed. When it had set down, she sat up in time to see Liam jogging from between the trees, dragging a man's body behind him.

One.

Adam hopped up and headed for him.

Pronto came over to her, and Roxie hugged her dog for a second before she stood. Every movement was labored, but she pushed through the struggle and did it anyway.

Liam let go of the man's pant leg and met her halfway, holding her elbows. "Carim is gone."

"What do you mean?" She couldn't talk loud enough to be heard over the helicopter, so she mostly mouthed the words.

"I didn't kill him. He was knocked out." Liam frowned. "Now he's gone."

"Gone." She looked around, shivering. Why did it seem like Carim might be watching? That was crazy. He'd probably run as far and as fast as he could as soon as he realized the plan was over.

Roxie squared her shoulders and drew on that well of divine peace in her soul.

Lord, help us.

"Come on. Let's get you to the hospital." Liam led her over, holding her up.

Adam had Darwish over his shoulder, flopped the guy into the helicopter, and climbed in. Pronto hopped up into the helicopter after him.

Liam helped her, and they slid onto the bench seat. He put his boots up on the dead guy's back. "Started with you being dead. Ends with you being dead."

Roxie smiled a little. It was true enough.

As far as she was concerned, it started with her and Liam being very much alive—and in love with each other, even if they hadn't been able to admit it. Or do anything about it.

And it was going to end with them being alive. Together.

She turned to him and put her palms on his cheeks. She tugged with the strength she had, and he leaned close. Roxie mouthed one word.

"Forever."

TWENTY

Liam paced the hall outside the room where the doctor was checking on Roxie, holding the phone tight to his ear. "Yeah, Mom. It's all good."

He couldn't help the tears that pricked his eyes.

Things could have ended so much worse than chaos. Crime up and down the coast, borne of panic. No bombs. No nuclear explosions.

They hadn't saved every bit of evil from happening, but they had saved a lot of people in the end.

"I'm so glad, honey. When I'm back in Benson, I'll come visit. Or you and Roxie should come and see me."

Liam smiled. "We do need a vacation. Although, that's also what started this whole thing."

He wasn't ready to chuckle about it yet, but the day would come. What he needed to do was find somewhere quiet to lift up prayers of gratitude for how God had guided them. He'd saved them. Enabled them to do the job and provided the resources they'd needed for success.

Forever.

He wanted to know what Roxie meant by that, but soon after she'd said it, she ran out of energy. He'd ended up carrying her off the chopper even though Adam wanted to do it.

Speaking of...

The rough looking Vanguard operative strode down the hall toward Liam, flanked by two of his men.

"I'll let you go." His mom said, "Love you, honey."

"You too, Mom." Liam ended the call.

Adam lifted his chin. "How is she?"

"Bruised throat." It had looked nasty, but she was breathing. "We'll find out the rest when the doctor is done."

Adam nodded.

"And the first nuke we disabled?"

"Landed at NORAD. Just like I said." As if Liam had been doubting him, and he had something to prove.

Liam held out his hand.

Adam clasped it.

"Thanks."

They shook, then let go.

Liam looked at his brother-in-law's men. "Thank you all for your help."

They nodded.

"Where are you guys off to next?"

Adam said, "The Famous Ones got a lead on something. Sounds like they want our help."

Liam said, "Stay safe." He figured they weren't going to disclose the mission or their whereabouts, so he didn't ask. "You're welcome to stay. Tell your sister you're leaving."

Adam looked at the door.

"She'll want to say bye."

He cleared his throat. "Yeah."

Thankfully, the doctor came out of the room right then. Liam wasn't sure how long he'd have managed to keep Adam there. The guy seemed almost nervous to face his sister.

Liam had no doubt that Roxie would ease those fears.

She wanted her brother in her life.

"How is she, Doc?"

The doctor said, "You're the husband?"

He nodded.

"She's tough. There's a lot of laryngeal swelling, and some warning signs to watch for, but she'll heal." He said, "I heard what you guys did. Thank you for your service." He looked at Liam, then at Adam and his guys. "All of you."

Liam cleared his throat. "Thanks, Doc."

The medic wandered off. Adam didn't move.

Liam reached over and squeezed the back of his neck. "Go." He gave Roxie's brother a little shove into the room.

Adam headed for the bed, where Roxie lay back on the pillows.

Liam had never seen anyone more beautiful than her, even how pale she was compared to the red marks on her neck. Even if she needed sleep, and so did he. They needed two weeks on a beach with no people and maybe only Pronto for miles around.

The dog was currently on Dakota's hospital bed, all the way down the hall, where she'd jumped up as soon as she saw the taskforce boss.

Roxie reached out a hand, and Adam took it. Tears rolled down her cheeks.

Everything in him wanted to go over to her. Instead, Liam stayed where he was. Carim had escaped, so technically, this wasn't over. The taskforce needed a moment to bounce back, and they would be after him.

There would always be work to do.

He and Roxie could spend years fighting crime, chasing bad guys, and stopping deadly threats. Lord willing, they would have decades.

The promise of so much time felt like a gift that couldn't be quantified.

Right now, it felt like forever.

Forever.

He knew what she meant now.

"Don't be a stranger." Roxie let go of her brother's hand.

He leaned down and kissed her forehead, said something Liam couldn't hear. Roxie gave her brother a soft smile, and he strode out.

Her gaze settled on Liam.

For some reason, his feet didn't take him over there. He wanted to stay where he was and just take her in.

She said, "All good?"

Liam crossed the room and touched her cheeks. He leaned down, his lips close to hers. She pressed her lips to his, and it seemed as though everything in him clicked into place.

"Forever."

She smiled. "Let's talk about that wedding."

EPILOGUE

Two months later.

Roxie ran her hands over the dress that flowed down over her knees to the white flip flops she'd bought specially for today.

Olivia O'Connell, Liam's mom, parked the car outside the big house where Gage and Clare lived. "Ready?"

In the sense she had a dress on, her makeup was done, and she'd had her hair styled. "Yes."

"You're already married." Olivia grinned. "Girl, why are you nervous?"

Roxie was being ridiculous. "Sorry. Let's do this thang." She shoved the door open.

Olivia burst into laughter.

They walked together up the front path, where Clare opened the door looking amazing. Her baby on her hip. Motherhood had barely slowed her down, although she'd given the CEO position to Liam's teammate Jasper so that he worked alongside her, doing more of the day to day managerial tasks.

Destiny was busy setting up a company childcare facility in the building. Apparently, she was going to call it, "Tactical Butterflies." Whatever that meant.

"Come in." Clare stepped back, opening the door wide. "They're ready for you."

Her entryway was bigger than Roxie's first apartment.

Destiny stepped in from a side room.

"Olivia and I will leave you to it." Clare closed the door—so Roxie couldn't make a run for it—and she and Liam's mom left her alone.

Roxie looked down at her dress. *This is ridiculous.* Why had she thought it was a good idea to wear this and stand up in front of everyone? They were only going to do a kind of re-commitment thing. People had flown in from other parts of the country. Even some team from Last Chance County, a group of rough looking guys everyone called "Chevalier." It turned out their leader was Liam's cousin of all things. There had been invitations. Presents. Food.

The whole thing was nuts.

"You look beautiful."

She looked up. Destiny had a summer dress on, cut to flow over her baby bump. The one she now had both hands on. Cradling her child already. Protecting her baby from whatever might come.

Tears pricked Roxie's eyes.

She lifted her chin and looked at the ceiling, blinking. Ruining her makeup by crying was *not* part of the plan.

"I'm sorry! I didn't mean to make you cry!" Destiny rushed over.

Roxie gave her friend a hug.

"I'm sorry I didn't call you."

Roxie had to chuckle. She'd been so mad, licking her wounds—protecting herself. "I didn't call *you*. And I'm sorry for that."

Destiny leaned back, swiping under her eyes. "Let's go out for lunch. Dinner. A girls spa day. Something."

"Anything." Roxie gave her another hug. "I'd like that."

Two men strode down the hall, wearing suits. Niall and Josh. She said, "Everything okay?"

Niall nodded.

Josh said, "We came to walk you out."

Niall elbowed him. "Down the aisle."

"Oh," Destiny said. "Blake and Jasper were talking about doing that for you." She looked around. "I wonder where they are?"

Simon and Peter, twins who might be identical but couldn't be more different, came into the lobby. Both had slacks and collared shirts but had evidently drawn the line at suits.

Simon's hair had grown out and now fell over his ears. "Need someone to—"

"—walk you down the aisle?" Peter finished the question.

"We're doing that." Niall frowned at them.

Bob Davis, her former boss at Vanguard, and Olivia's boyfriend, apparently, appeared. "Hey, Roxie—"

Simon said, "We already offered, so don't."

"Oh." Destiny looked around again.

The front door opened.

Roxie's brother stepped inside, a fresh cut above

his right eyebrow that had been secured with a tiny butterfly bandage. He spotted her. "Need someone to give you away?"

Roxie stared at him.

Then she burst out laughing.

She'd gone from having no one to stand with her, no family, and no one to give her away, to having more offers than she knew what to do with.

She wound her arm in her brother's and looked at her friends. "Sorry, guys."

Simon looked at his twin, Niall, Josh, and Bob. "Does this make us bridesmaids?"

Josh frowned. "Guess we should go first, then. You know, down the aisle."

Roxie chuckled. "You aren't going to..."

They all trailed away down the hall. Destiny followed them, giggling.

She looked up at Adam.

He said, "I heard the taskforce is being sent to D.C. for a few months."

She nodded. Current consensus was that after taking down Darwish and stopping such a huge potential attack, they were victims of their own success.

The hunt for Carim was ongoing.

She said, "Let's do this thang."

He grinned. "Okay, dork."

They walked through the house, out onto the patio, and she got a look at the backyard. Lights had been hung around the perimeter. After it got dark, it would look gorgeous. The rows and rows of chairs were full—at least a hundred people, all of whom had turned to watch pairs of men in their wedding-best clothes walk down the aisle.

Someone chuckled.

A dog barked.

Then another. Then another.

There were at least ten dogs in the yard, stationed around the perimeter with their handlers from the Search and Rescue training center.

Vanguard.

The taskforce.

The Benson PD.

Her brother and his team.

She had so much family she didn't know what to do with.

"Thought we were gonna do this *thang*."

"Shut up." Roxie chuckled, and they started down the aisle to a beautiful song she didn't know. She spotted Olivia just as her mother-in-law dabbed at a tear with a tissue.

Up at the front, the pastor from their Benson church stood with his Bible.

Liam to one side, Blake, Jasper, and Gage beside him. Their former teammate, Dakota Masterson, was supposed to have been here but had signed up to fight wildfires for the summer in Montana. He was currently in training, so they were planning to meet up in the fall. She couldn't wait to meet him and hear his story. She wanted to tell their former SWAT buddy Dakota all about her boss, the spitfire female Dakota.

On her side, Simon and Peter stood with Niall and Josh. Four men, with Destiny in front of them. Her "bridesmaids." Roxie grinned.

Adam walked her all the way to Liam.

Roxie kissed her brother's cheek and would've sworn he blushed.

He left her there, and she turned to Liam.

"Hey, beautiful."

Roxie stared at him a lot, listened to the preacher —kind of—and repeated what she was supposed to say while Destiny chuckled.

Finally, the preacher said, "Ladies and gentlemen—"

Roxie spun around and slammed into Liam who apparently had the same idea. She slid her arms around his neck while he pulled her to him.

He leaned in for a kiss.

She whispered, "I'm pregnant."

His whole body stilled, and he stared at her with so much wonder.

"Oops?" She hadn't been planning on it, and only just figured out why she'd felt this low-grade nausea the past two weeks. "I guess right after the cabin burned down, I kind of forgot about the whole birth control thing. Then you were dead. Then you were alive again, and it didn't occur to me to go to the pharmacy, since we were busy finding nukes and kicking bad guys' butts."

Someone barked a laugh.

She bit her lip.

Liam bent slightly, wrapped his arm under her behind, and lifted her into the air. He spun her around.

Roxie squealed and held on for dear life.

Liam yelled, "We're having a baby!"

The audience of people stood, clapping and laughing. Cheering.

Finally, he lowered her. He gave her the sweetest kiss of her life, one she would never forget. *Thank You.* It went on so long, people started to laugh louder. Someone whistled. Liam lifted his head and smiled in a way that pricked more tears in her eyes. "Forever."

She touched his cheeks. "I know."

Pronto barked.

She grinned. "Let's party."

I hope you enjoyed *Forever - Part 2*, please consider leaving a review, it really helps others find their next read!

Turn the page to learn more about where it all began in *Allegiance*, book 1 of Benson First Responders.

A disgraced cop hiding a dangerous secret.

Police Detective Lucas Westbrook has served his whole career under the shadow of his mother's betrayal. Only his faith keeps him from crossing the line or becoming the cop everyone assumes he is. This time there's no escaping the connection between his deepest pain and the case on his desk.

Caught in a tangled web between friend and foe, Lucas will protect Freya. For as long as it takes to close the case—and find out what could be between them.

Find out more and get started today at: https://authorlisaphillips.com/product/allegiance/

And if you've been following the Benson First Responder series, continue the story with *Duplicity!*

A score to settle.

Vanguard technical specialist Simon Olson has spent years working to make up for the mistakes he made. With his twin about to marry the love of his life, Simon has one last job to do, and he'll be able to let go enough to move on without the past hanging over his head. Too bad it means going to high school for the first time...as a teacher.

A battle for truth.

Officer Catalina Alvarez is the East Benson High school resource officer. Even with the legacy of police service in her blood, it still seems as if everyone expects her to prove herself. Cat has found her place walking the mean streets...uh, halls...of high school. Still, the death of her partner and conviction the kid who confessed to shooting them both never quite fit.

If she finds the real killer, she'll finally be able to let the past rest in peace.

As Simon hunts for the server hosting the criminal technology he invented, his new boss at Vanguard discovers what he's doing and gives him an ultimatum. Cat is called to the scene of a missing teen girl, one of several abducted recently, allowing Vanguard and the police to join forces to fight a new threat—putting Cat and Simon in the middle when it all breaks open.

Simon finally gets his shot at taking down the communication network. But will the price of victory be too high?

Find out more at: https://authorlisaphillips.com/product/duplicity/

ABOUT THE AUTHOR

Find out more about Lisa Phillips at her website, where you'll discover more romantic suspense fan-favorite series and heart-pounding thriller novels.
https://authorlisaphillips.com

If you loved this book, please consider sharing about it on social media, or leaving a review on Lisa's website. Your review will help others find great books to entertain and encourage them!

For a FREE novel from Lisa Phillips, scan the QR code below with your phone camera to connect to Lisa's newsletter and be the first to hear about sales, new books, and recommendations for your TBR pile.

facebook.com/authorlisaphillips

instagram.com/lisaphillipsbks

bookbub.com/authors/lisa-phillips